The Knights of St. John

By PAUL L. ANDERSON

THE CUB ARRIVES

HALF-PINT SHANNON

WITH THE EAGLES

A SLAVE OF CATILINE

FOR FREEDOM AND FOR GAUL

THE KNIGHTS OF ST. JOHN

HE SWUNG UP THE SCIMITAR.

[page 82]

The Knights of St. John

By

Paul L. Anderson

Illustrations by
M. Painter Duhring

D. APPLETON AND COMPANY
New York :: 1932 :: London

To

CONTENTS

Contents

ILLUSTRATIONS

CHAPTER I

Of the Cells of the Inquisition; and Jehan Parisot de la Vallette

IT was in July of the year 1564 of Our Blessed Redeemer that the caravel in which I took passage from France to the Island of Malta was wrecked in a storm, and I was cast ashore on the coast of Spain, not far from Barcelona. I had journeyed from London to Paris for my induction into the Order of the Knights Hospitallers of St. John of Jerusalem, and with me had gone a Spanish nobleman, Don Diego de Espinosa, who joined the Order at the same time as myself. The reason for this shall be duly set forth later, but for the present let me say only that Don Diego and I were separated in the wreck, a matter of no great grief to me, since I mistrusted his smooth Spanish courtesy, thought him apt to be treacherous behind a polished manner, and found his Castilian pride offensive.

Up to the time of our being overtaken by the storm, the journey was pleasant enough, but about the middle of the fatal morning, when we were some miles off the coast, the sky grew dark, and in the distance levin-flashes could be seen against the slate-gray clouds. There was much crying back and forth among the seamen, with running to and fro to make all secure, and while this went forward the great clouds mounted ever more and more swiftly to the zenith, then spread like a vast dome over the entire heavens. Gradually the thunder became audible, growing rapidly to a terrific crashing uproar that was well-nigh continuous, battering down the senses and stunning us with its violence, so that even in my fear I was reminded of those lines of Vergilius Maro: "Black night broods o'er the sea; from pole to pole rolls the thunder, and the air flames with incessant fires."

Then with a hissing roar the rain struck us, not in drops nor yet in lancing lines, but in a solid sheet, like some vast waterfall, and at the same moment the wind caught our vessel, snapped off the masts, flung the ship on its beam-ends, whirled it about, and drove it, reeling and plunging, toward the distant coast. Some of the mariners were carried away in that first dreadful onslaught of the gale, but there was naught could be done for them; the huge seas were breaking over our decks with giant masses of green water and white, swirling foam, so that one who lost hold of cordage or bulwark was from that moment doomed beyond all hope. I tried, indeed, to catch one wretched man as he was swept by me, but though I gripped his jerkin, so great was the water's pull that the stout leather tore apart and he was washed away.

Thus, helpless before the mighty power of the gale, we were driven shoreward, the vessel at length smashing with terrible violence on a hidden rock. My grip was wrenched loose and I was flung overboard, to be hurled about, now under, now above the water, until in contempt the waves tossed me on the sand. Swimming with all my strength, I managed to avoid being either crushed or carried out to sea, and finally, bruised, exhausted, and aching in every limb, I crawled to safety beyond the licking surges. For some time I rested here, then got to my feet and searched along the shore, if haply there might be someone to whom I could carry help.

There were but half a dozen or so survivors of the wreck, I being—as I then thought—the only one of noble birth. The others were ordinary seamen of the French nation, who joined me in the search, and having assured ourselves that our companions were beyond human aid we took our way through the storm to. a nearby village. The weather's violence had kept the townspeople indoors, so none knew of the wreck, and we roused much interest when we presented ourselves at the inn. Speaking Spanish nearly as fluently as my native English, I was able to set forth the plight of my companions and myself, whereupon most of those in the hostelry, as well as a great part of the town, left hot-foot for the shore, to profit by any wreckage the waves might cast up.

However, there remained the inn-keeper and his wife, together with three or four loutish drawers and grooms, and among them they built up a roaring fire for us to dry ourselves, and brought us hot food and wine. The place was dirty and rude, but not much inferior to our English country inns, and I was able to rest in comfort after my battle with the waves; I may say without vanity that only a strong swimmer could have come living through that surf, and it had taxed even my strength to do so. And what with the wine, the heat of the fire, and the fatigue, I found myself dozing, and presently relaxed in my chair and slept.

I must have slept for some hours, for on waking I found that many of the flotsam-hunters had returned, and the common room was filled with a crowd of rough Catalonian fishermen, displaying their trove and arguing loudly, with frequent oaths and gesticulations. They were drinking the harsh wine of the country, but at my summons the landlord brought me a smoother southern vintage, and finding myself rested and refreshed—in those days I enjoyed the quick resilience of youth—I amused myself with sipping the wine, listening to the discussion, and watching the assembled folk. It was a scene meriting the pencil of the great Tintoretto, with the firelight and the flickering lamps—for night had drawn down by now—casting strange dancing shadows on the walls and illumining the rude faces and forms, or picking out here and there some glinting eye or glittering pendant.

In time, though, I tired of it, and rose, calling the landlord to show me to bed, when a remark, cutting through a chance silence, took my notice.

"I will give ten pounds of wax candles to Our Lady of Monte Serrado," said one of the men, a trifle better dressed than the others, holding up a necklace of gems that flashed white and red and green. "The Holy Image has this day granted me undreamed wealth. I took these from the bosom of a lady of quality whom the waves cast ashore. She had no further use for them," he added, with a brutal chuckle.

There had been a French lady on our vessel, journeying to Italy, but the waves swept her overboard when first we struck, and in the welter of seas and wreckage I was unable to reach her with aid; doubtless it was she whom this ghoul had stripped and searched. My gorge rose at his brutality, at the thought of his great coarse paws handling her delicate body, but it would have been madness to provoke a quarrel in the circumstances. However, I could not refrain from a trifling sarcasm, and said:

"Give thanks to the Most Holy Virgin, my friend. It is She, and not Her image, that has sent you this good fortune."

A shocked silence followed, like that of a dovecote when a goshawk passes over, and all eyes were bent on me. Shrugging my shoulders, I turned to follow the landlord from the room, but my way was barred by a huge, red-faced, burly fellow who jumped from his chair and strode between me and the door.

"Not so fast, young sir," he said. "Do I understand you to hold that Our Lady of Monte Serrado does not work miracles?"

I had no great liking for either his face or his manner, but I replied, courteously:

"It seems to me that miracles and such favors are from the Mother of Our Blessed Redeemer, and are not wrought by Her images, which are but of stone or wood."

"Enough!" he answered. "This is heresy most vile. Know, young man, that I am a Familiar of the Holy Office, and am powered to arrest all heretics, wherever found. You must go with me."

Here was a fine state of affairs! If I had escaped the sea only to fall into the hands of the Inquisition, I had but exchanged one fate for a worse one—the frying-pan for the fire, though so far as fire goes, the jest was over-near the truth to be humorous. I

6

had cast aside my sword in the battle with the waves, but instantly I snatched my dagger from its sheath and drove at the officer's body, meaning to slay him and escape in the confusion. Unfortunately for me, he was wearing chain mail under his doubtlet, and the blade shattered, though the force of the blow sent him back against the door. But ere I could get past him, the landlord flung himself at my legs, bringing me down, something descended with stunning force on my head, and all was black.

When I came to myself, I was lying on a rough pallet in a stone-walled room, which was lighted only by two small, iron-barred windows high up in one wall. There was a damp chill in the air, and the place smelled musty and sour, with a taint of foulness in its aroma. My head ached slightly, but I sat up and looked around, to see another cot like mine, on which other sat a man in an attitude of despair, elbows on knees and face in hands.

"Where am I?" I asked, and he raised his head and looked at me. By his dress and features and manner he was evidently a gentleman of Spain.

"You are in the cárceles secretas, the secret cells of the Holy Office," he told me. "God pity you!" he added, sympathetically.

Then I remembered, and my blood turned cold and my throat suddenly went dry.

7

A pitcher stood on a table against one wall, and stepping over to it I found it full of water.

"May I?" I asked, and he responded, graciously: "Of course. Half of it is yours, in any case."

I took a deep drink and felt better, then returned to my cot.

"How long am I likely to remain here?" I inquired, whereat he smiled in bitterness.

"Until you recant your heresy. Or if you persistently deny your guilt, and are judged an impenitente negativo, until you are relaxed to the secular arm and depart this world in the flames of an auto de fé."

I shuddered at the prospect.

"I am no heretic," I said. "As God sees me, I have no thought that is not purely Catholic."

He laughed a short and mirthless laugh.

"Convince the Inquisitor of that. I myself am a good Catholic, but on some foolish quibble of dogma I have been held here during four years and seven months, sin communicación."

I was shocked at this.

"You mean you cannot get word to your friends?" I asked.

"I cannot even learn if my wife and children still live. I shall know nothing of them, nor they of me, unless by chance we catch a glimpse of each other when, wearing the san benito, I take part in

8

the melancholy procession to the stake." I shivered again, not altogether from the chill of the dungeon. "Nay, more," he went on. "In all that time I have not been permitted to hear Mass, nor even to partake of the Blessed Sacrament. Nor shall I, unless dying, when a priest may be admitted to give me extreme unction." I was struck with horror at such refinement of cruelty; this was to damn a man's soul as well as his body!

Presently, with a deep sigh, my companion in misfortune rose from his seat.

"It is vain to think of these things," he remarked. "That way lies madness. Can you cook?"

Surprised at so irrelevant a question, I shook my head.

"You had best learn," he told me. "They bring us food on Thursdays and Sundays, but we must cook it ourselves. And if I am taken away, you may find yourself in evil case unless you know how to prepare it. I knew nothing of the art when I was brought here, but another victim taught me." He did not say what had become of the other, and I forbore to ask. He produced from one corner a brazier, charcoal, bellows, tinder, and flint and steel. "At least you can kindle the fire," he said, "while I make ready the victuals."

I set the coals glowing, and he cooked and served what he called an olla podrida, a not untoothsome dish resembling a stew, though somewhat highly seasoned for my English palate. My companion explained, however, that apart from Spanish taste, this seasoning was necessary to disguise the flavor of the meat, which often kept but ill from Sunday till Thursday, especially in the warmth of summer.

"Still," he said, "while the meat is fresh we can be more gentle with the garlic and peppers, in deference to your liking."

While we ate, several rats and a toad or two came looking for food, which my companion gave them.

"They are harmless," he answered my look of disgust. "And the time may come, as it has come to me, when you will be glad of their company."

To make a long story short, we were for three months together in this dungeon, becoming no little attached to each other, until one day men came and took my companion away. We bade each other farewell, and I have never seen him since, nor could I extract from the carcelero, the jailer, any slightest hint as to his fate; to this day I have no knowledge of what befell him—though I can shrewdly guess. God rest his soul! He was Martin Guevera, a merchant of the town, and a worthy and courteous gentleman, though not of noble blood.

Left alone, I tried to find out when I would be brought to trial, but could learn nothing on that score. Also, on his semi-weekly visits with food, I tried to corrupt the jailer, whom I found to waver between his greed for gold and his fear of his masters. I had some coins in a belt around my waist, and I used to show these to the man, clinking them together and letting them shine in the dim light of the cell, polishing them on my sleeve until they gleamed as though new minted, while he eyed them with a comical mixture of covetousness and dread— that is, it would have been comical had not my need been so dire.

"One ... two ... three ... four ..." I would count. "Eight ... nine ... ten. Ten golden angels for pen and paper. And another ten to carry a message to the nearest Commandery of the Knights of St. John. Eh? Who desires wealth in return for a kind act?" For twenty angels was indeed wealth to a man like him.

Then his lip would quiver and his hand reach out to the gold, and he would turn and flee as though the devil himself pursued.

At length his resistance broke, and one day, after setting down the food, he placed before me pen, ink, and paper.

"I have told them that you asked for these in order to draw up your defence," he said. "Do so, for each sheet of paper is counted, and must be restored. To your own use, this. . . ." He lowered his voice and glanced fearfully around, then from under his doublet brought a grimy scrap, the title-page torn from a much-handled copy of the Orlando Innamorato. "For yourself, this . . . and I will carry your message. There are Knights of the Order, I hear, at Monte Serrado—what you call Montserrat—though that is not a Commandery. But you must swear on this crucifix to protect me if I am discovered."

I laid my hand on the crucifix.

"In the Presence of Our Blessed Saviour, I swear it," I assured him. "Wait!"

I penned a brief note:

"A Knight of St. John, held prisoner in the cells of the Holy Office in—" I looked up. "We are in Barcelona?" The jailer nodded. "—in Barcelona. Help, in the name of God and St. John!"

Folding the message, I gave it to him, then counted out twenty golden angels and handed them over also, saying:

"May your hand wither and become as naught if you betray me!"

He cringed at the threat, but took the gold, replying:

"I will not play you false."

And on those words he departed, leaving me with at least a gleam of hope.

That was on Sunday, and for two more days I

was left to the society of my rats and toads—quite tame and friendly they were, and not uncompanionable, when I had got over my first dislike—and on Wednesday the cell door was unlocked and swung back. I leaped up, expecting to see deliverance, but my heart sank as I was confronted by three Familiars, under command of the Fiscal of the Holy Office.

"Come!" said this last, and perforce I followed, the Familiars guarding me at side and rear.

Down a short corridor we marched, then into the audience-chamber, a large room hung all about with black, save that opposite the door was an anteroom hidden by a celosia, a lattice from behind which a witness, himself unseen, could identify a prisoner. In front of this lattice, and some eight or ten feet from it, was a long table, covered with a black velvet cloth on which a cross was worked in gold; and behind the table sat three men, robed from head to foot in black. At one end sat a notary, with writing materials before him, but it was the central figure of the three who caught and held my attention. The other two were, I afterward learned, the Calificadores, ecclesiastics who would pass on acts and words as to whether or not they constituted heresy, and there was about them some suggestion of humanity. But the central one—!

Bolt upright he sat, not leaning back in his chair,

his clasped hands resting on the edge of the table, nor was there in his thin, ascetic face or cold black eyes one faintest hint of mercy. His high-arched nose jutted forth like the beak of some fierce bird of prey, and so tight was the skin drawn over the bridge that it shone as though polished; from the corners of his nose deeply graven lines ran down to the lipless, cruel mouth; a square chin thrust forth above a sinewy neck; and a thousand wrinkles seamed the roughened skin of his face. But worst of all were the eyes. Black, fathomless, red-rimmed, they blazed from deep caverns overhung by bristling hair, nor was there in them any possible relenting; they seemed the deadly, unblinking orbs of some venomous reptile. By long years of self-mortification and by long gazing on human agony this man had eradicated from his heart all sympathy, and I knew that I was in the remorseless grip of a fanatic.

For perhaps a minute he stared at me and I stared back, while my stomach grew sick and my hands and feet turned icy cold. Then at last he spoke, and it was strange to hear such a voice issue from those lips, for its tones were rich, deep, and musical, vibrating as sweetly as the notes of some great harp.

"Your name?" he asked.

"Sir Richard Ayresford."

"Earthly titles are naught before the Holy Of-

fice. Write down 'Richard Ayresford,' " This last
to the notary, who bowed. Then to me:

"Of England?"

"Yes."

"Your age?"

"Twenty-two."

"Are you of the true faith, or a heretic?"

"As God sees me, I am of the true faith."

"Are your parents living?"

"My mother died three years agone; my father,
six."

"How did they die?"

"My mother, of the sweating sickness; my
father—" I hesitated.

"Speak out!"

"He was burned at Smithfield, by order of the
late Queen Mary of England."

"He was, then, a heretic?"

"So it was said. But he was a good man."

"There can be no good in a heretic. The Evil
One does at times give a seeming of good, that he
may lead astray those who put their faith in out-
ward appearance. But you say you are not a
heretic?"

"My mother taught me; I am a true son of Holy
Church."

One of the Calificadores spoke in a low tone to
the Inquisitor, who nodded and replied:

"This agrees with the word we had. Is the accused identified as Richard Ayresford, of England?"

The notary got up and passed behind the celosia, returning in a few moments to say:

"He is."

I wondered who there could be in Barcelona to identify me. It could not be one of the people from the inn, for they did not know my name . . . or had I given it? I could not remember. Possibly one of the seamen from the vessel. Or it might be that the Holy Office had sent to England for some priest who knew me. All all events, I could inquire.

"May I know who accuses me?" I asked, to which the Inquisitor answered, emotionless:

"No."

And that discussion was closed. Had I but known the truth, as I learned it months afterward—still, what difference could it have made? In point of fact, none, so regrets are vain.

There was a whispered conference, then the Inquisitor resumed:

"On the eighteenth day of this month, in the presence of witnesses, you were heard to say that the miracles wrought by Our Lady of Monte Serrado were wrought by the Holy Virgin Herself, and not by the image. Do you hold this belief?"

"It seems to me," I replied, truthfully, "that

16

miracles must come from the Mother of God, and not from a figure of stone or wood made in Her likeness. I cannot see that this is heresy; certainly it detracts nothing from Her power or glory."

"It is not for you to judge whether or not it constitutes heresy; that will be decided by those wiser than you."

"But—"

"Be silent!"

Another whispered conference, then:

"Richard Ayresford, by your own admission you stand convicted of heretical belief and utterance. You will be allowed seven days for meditation and repentance, then if you refuse to recant you will be put to the trial by the garrucha. Should you still remain obdurate, you will be relaxed to the secular arm as a gangrenous spot in the body politic, to be purified by fire. Remove him!"

I was escorted back to my cell, locked in, and left alone with my thoughts.

They were far from pleasant reflections. It seemed incredible that the Holy Office should torture and burn a man for so slight a divergence of belief, and I tried to comfort myself with the thought that they would but frighten me, and let me go. And then I remembered those who had suffered and died for less than this—remembered, too, the merciless face of the Inquisitor—and my heart sank within me. No, there was no hope that way.

What was the garrucha? I did not know—but it would unquestionably be horrible. And I proceeded to imagine all manner of frightful tortures; if common malefactors were treated to the rack, the boots, and the thumbkins, surely the Inquisition would have something extraordinary in the nature of torment to offer. And following that, what? Why, pardi! the long months of waiting, and at last the san benito, that coarse tunic of yellow linen with red crosses on back and breast; the solemn procession; the eager crowds; the stake, the chains, and the fire. Well, God give me strength to endure it! Better men than I—yes, even my own father, than whom no finer ever lived—had died that way, though he had been spared the preliminary torture which was to be mine. Still, I had heard it said that if one could inhale the flames his end was quick.

I do not know why I did not go mad during that awful week, unless by the pure grace of God. Certainly I prayed much to Him, as well as to the Blessed Redeemer, to His Mother, and to the holy saints. At times the Tempter crept into my heart, whispering: "Why not profess repentance? It is but a matter of words; it is but saying that the image performs the miracles. And after all, how know you that such is not the case? Wiser men than you have said so! And thus will you escape the garrucha, the stake, and the flame." Then I would fall on my knees and cry aloud: "Oh, Most Blessed Virgin, Mother of Our Lord, let me not deny Thee!" And I would feel the strength, the aid, that She sent to my harassed soul.

At times the thought would come to me that the Knights of St. John would rescue me in time, that they would not abandon a comrade in distress, and with that the Tempter would whisper low: "But what can they do? What earthly might can withstand the Holy Office? What of the others who have felt the flame? Had they no friends, no protectors? How of the men of wealth, the grandees of Spain, the noble matrons, the lovely maids? Not riches nor power, not station nor beauty, could save their venerable heads, their white bodies, from the fire! Are you worthier than they? Best make submission, my friend!"

Then I would defy him, saying: "It is not in the honor of a Knight of St. John to lie, even for life itself." And he would answer: "What is honor? A word! What will your honor profit you when your joints crack under the garrucha, when the fire licks shrivelling along your limbs?" And he would chuckle, adding: "Wait till you feel the flame! And then it will be too late! Too late!"

I came to envy the rats and toads that lived with

me. Base things though they were, at least they were not tortured by the agonies that stormed my soul, and before the week was out I would gladly have changed places with any of them. It seemed to me strange to think that within a few weeks or months I would be naught but a heap of ashes, scattered by the winds, while they would live on, perchance wondering dimly what had become of him who used to feed them, but content when another wretched man should take my place and fling them scraps. But my sufferings did not make me harsh with these poor companions; the more I was tortured by men, the gentler I grew toward my little friends, feeding and petting them, and liking to fancy that they regarded me with dumb brute sympathy. And so the dreadful week wore on to the final day.

Early in the morning of the eighth day the door of my cell was flung back, and I rose, my heart leaping to the hope of rescue. But it was only the grim Familiars whom I had seen before, and now they bound my wrists behind my back, then urged me out of the cell. We did not go to the audience-chamber, but turned in the other direction, marching along an echoing corridor of stone, down a flight of stairs, and so to an underground room, a dungeon whose iron door clanged shut behind me like that of a tomb. Here the Inquisitor waited, with three hard-faced and brutal men in attendance, and as I faced him he asked:

"Richard Ayresford, do you recant?"

My throat was so parched with terror of the awful fate before me that I could not answer, but shook my head, and he nodded to the men, saying:

"Do your duty."

And they advanced on me.

The dungeon was completely sealed, having no window or opening of any kind save the door by which I had entered; no cry of agony could pierce those walls, to reach the outer world. The room was about five paces square, built wholly of stone, with a vaulted ceiling perhaps ten feet high over the central part; and set in the masonry of wall and ceiling were several pulleys, a stout rope reeved through them. In one corner lay a pile of curious devices, including a ladder-like contrivance some eight feet long, an earthen jar, and various cords and sticks. But it soon appeared that I was not concerned with these, for the torturers led me to the center of the room, tied my ankles together, and after assuring themselves that my wrists were firmly bound, attached to them the end of the rope which depended from the ceiling.

Then as the men hauled on the end of the rope, lifting my arms behind me and gradually hoisting me from the floor, I learned what the garrucha is—

learned, too, the agony it brings. At first it was not bad, but as the minutes passed there came into my shoulder-joints an ache that rose from dull pain to the most sharp and stinging torture, and this torture grew and swelled until it filled the whole world, blurring the stone floor before my down-turned eyes, blurring the sound of the Miserere which the Inquisitor slowly intoned, and bringing the sweat to my forehead and well-nigh forcing a groan from my clenched teeth. Three times he repeated the whole of that psalm, from the beginning; "Miserere mei, Deus," to the end, then at his nod the torturers lowered me to the floor.

"Do you repent and recant your error?" he asked, and I shook my head. I was wholly beyond speech —but at least I had endured in silence.

He said a few words, and one of the men came forward and tied an iron weight of perhaps twenty pounds to my ankles, then they hoisted me again.

"Slowly, slowly," the Inquisitor cautioned them. "If you lift suddenly, the pain departs too soon."

So they hoisted me very slowly, the agony growing sharper and sharper as my feet cleared the floor. The first time, they had lifted only until my toes could barely touch the flagging, but now my feet were a yard above the stones, and I twisted slowly about as the rope unwound. Fiercer and fiercer grew the pain, but I ground my teeth in silence and waited for the third Miserere to end. At length the final words were spoken, and with a little surge of pride that I had not yielded I waited the sign which would bring a temporary relief from the torture. But I had exulted too soon, for at the Inquisitor's nod the men, instead of lowering me to the floor, let me drop about two feet, then snubbed sharply on the rope, checking my fall. So frightful and so unexpected was the stab of pain which shot through me that I flung back my head and gasped in agony, and a fleeting look of satisfaction swept for an instant over the Inquisitor's face. Then I was lowered to the floor and again he asked:

"Do you repent and recant your error?" And again I shook my head.

Another weight was attached to my ankles, but just as the men were about to hoist, there came a thundering on the iron door. The Inquisitor raised his hand, and indicated that the door be unlocked. It was hurled rudely back and into the cell there strode a tall, broad-shouldered man, plainly dressed, wearing high riding-boots of tan leather, and over all a black mantle with the white, eight-pointed cross of St. John. At his left side hung a long, straight sword with jeweled hilt, and a Toledo dagger balanced it on the right. He was perhaps sixty-five years old, or more, and his full, square beard, once

brown, was now gray, his high-domed head nearly
bald, but for all his age his motions were alert and
vigorous, and his rather kindly face wore an expression of authority as his piercing brown eyes glanced
about the cell. Three others followed him, dressed
as he was, but much younger, and the four halted
in the middle of the room, the older man's eyes
coming to rest on the Inquisitor.

"I learn," said the new-comer, "that you hold in
your cárceles one of the Knights of St. John. Is
this he?" And he motioned toward me.

"Who are you?" demanded the Inquisitor. "And
by what right do you come between the Holy Office
and a heretic?"

"I am Jehan Parisot de la Vallette, Grand Master
of the Knights Hospitallers of St. John of Jerusa-
lem," was the haughty reply. "Which tells you
both my name and my right." He turned to me.
"Are you the one who sent the message asking aid?"
I nodded feebly. "Release him!" said the Grand
Master, and his companions cut my bonds, then as
I tottered they caught me in their arms.

The Familiars stepped forward as though to in-
terfere, but a glance from la Vallette froze them
in their tracks.

"Your name?" the Grand Master inquired of me,
and taking a deep breath I gathered my strength
and replied:

"Richard Ayresford, sir."

"A Knight of Justice?"

I shook my head.

"No. An Associate of the Order," I answered.

"Where were you accepted?"

"At the Commandery of Paris."

"The Knight Commander?"

"Pierre de la Nouë."

"Your sponsors?"

"The Chevalier Jehan de Rohan and Sir Oliver Starkey."

"So? Be careful what you say; Sir Oliver is my personal secretary."

"So I understood, yes. He will vouch for me."

La Vallette stepped to me, turned his back on the Inquisitor, and flung his left arm about my shoulders, extending his right hand. With difficulty I laid mine in it, giving him the grip of an Associate Knight, and he kissed me on both cheeks. Then stepping back, he unclasped his mantle and laid it over my shoulders. Turning to the Inquisitor, he said:

"Sir Richard Ayresford is under protection of the cross of St. John. It is not for you or any other to harm him."

Suddenly the Inquisitor blazed out in fury:

"Beware what you do, Jehan Parisot de la Vallette! Beware how you come between the Holy Office and Her victims! Beware lest you draw down upon yourself and upon your Order the fearful ban of excommunication! How will you answer to the Grand Inquisitor for this act?"

La Vallette stepped close to the Inquisitor, so fierce a flame in his brown eyes that the other shrank away.

"Let the Holy Office threaten earthly potentates," said la Vallette, his voice low and restrained, yet thrilling with power. "But understand once and for all, Sir Inquisitor, that the Grand Master of the Knights of St. John answers for his words and his deeds only to Our Father in Heaven, and to no earthly soul. I care less than naught for Fernando Valdés, the Grand Inquisitor, nor will His Holiness the Pope pronounce the ban of excommunication on one who is the chief bulwark of Christendom against the Moslem. Be warned! Meddle not with my children! Sir Richard Ayresford is my man, and none save I myself shall order him to discipline. Attempt to hinder me by word or act, and I will hang you to this devilish engine of yours and leave you here to die!" He turned to me. "Come, Sir Richard. You are for Malta?"

I bowed, not trusting myself to speak.

"It is well," the Grand Master went on. "Duty calls, and glory awaits you there. Our galley is at the wharf. Come!"

The Inquisitor snarled like an angry dog, but la

Vallette gave him no further attention, and with the younger knights most tenderly supporting me, we made our way from those gloomy halls into that freedom of air and sunlight of which I had so long despaired.

CHAPTER II

Of the Lady Alice Chauntrey; and How I
Set Forth to War

THE Grand Master, it appeared, had been in Spain on some business of the Order, and stopped for a few days at the famous monastery of Monte Serrado, to offer prayers at the shrine. There my message, after passing through sundry hands, was at last delivered to him, and he rode posthaste to Barcelona.

"Could I leave one of my men in the clutch of the Holy Office?" he asked, in telling me this. "How can I expect loyalty from them if I give it not in return?"

"But will it not bring trouble on you?" I inquired, a trifle anxiously. "I am told that the Grand Inquisitor is jealous beyond measure of his rights and privileges."

La Vallette chuckled softly, and the corners of his eyes broke into a thousand humorous wrinkles.

"Fret not your mind about that, Sir Richard," he answered. "His Most Catholic Majesty, Philip of Spain, is my good friend, and he will know how to answer Fernando Valdés."

We were on the Grand Master's galley, flying over the wine-dark sea toward Malta, and there were a score of Knights on board, all glad to welcome me, to aid me when necessary—for my shoulders were still lame from the garrucha, though by God's mercy they had not been twisted from the sockets—and one and all eager to hear how I had fallen victim to the Holy Office.

"Begin at the beginning, Sir Richard," begged Juan de la Mara. "Tell us of your boyhood as well, to beguile the journey; we have some four or five days to spend on the sea." He was a dark, eager youth of my own age, and I had taken an instant liking to him—the more, perhaps, since it was he who, with the Grand Master's nephew and the latter's comrade-in-arms, Polastra, had followed la Vallette into the torture-chamber. But de la Mara was an incurable romantic, sighing for the dead days of chivalry, and my cold northern blood could not keep pace with his flaming imagination. So now I shook my head and smiled, saying:

"Mine is no Odyssey of adventure. Humdrum and dull enough, save for the past few months. Still, if you would have it—"

So while the fifty clacking, splashing oars urged us on, and the swaying, sweaty backs of the Moslem galley-slaves gleamed like moist ivory in the sun, we of the Order sat under a canopy on the poop-

29

deck, and I told of my life and how I set out to serve Christendom and win renown. The Grand Master, indeed, was busy in his cabin, with de Monti, Admiral of the Order, and Sir Oliver Starkey (who had given me warm welcome), but de la Mara, the younger la Vallette, Polastra, the Chevalier de Miranda, and a dozen others paid me the compliment of listening with open ears.

I told of my family, descended from one of the Border houses, but now for many years loyal servants of the English king; of that dreadful day when my father died for conscience's sake at Smithfield; and of how my mother thereafter crept about the house, a stricken thing, until death ended her sufferings. I told of how I received knighthood at the hands of His Grace of Devonshire, and how in his train I met the Lady Alice Chauntrey, and became her willing—nay, adoring—slave, the captive of her bow and spear.

Indeed, she was a winsome creature, was Lady Alice, with her yellow hair, blue eyes, and creamy skin; with her dainty, fairy-like form, and her mouth that seemed made for man's delight but proved his torment. A coquette from the jeweled caul that enclosed her curly locks to the tips of her high-heeled shoes of Spanish leather, she alternately repelled and attracted me, drove me mad with jealousy, and when I was about to leave her, vowing that it

would be forever, then with a flashing smile and a
kindly word she would call me back, that I might
lay my heart once more at her feet and beg her
to trample on it. She knew no lack of admirers,
for all the young gallants of the court—and, to their
shame be it said, some of the married ones as well—
swarmed about her like flies round a honey-pot,
gladly riding the ten miles from London to Chauntrey Court on the chance of a smile and a word
from her lips. Sir John Eastern, Sir Philip Blaikie,
the young Viscount Falwyn—these and many others
sighed their devotion, drank her health, and worshipped the ground on which she trod, while she
beguiled them, teased them, laughed at them, lured
them on only to repel them, read and admired the
verses they wrote to her, and, in brief, drove them to
utter distraction. Two she seemed to favor somewhat; myself and one other, of whom more later.
For two long years I danced attendance on her,
swinging between the heaven of hope and the hell
of despair, until at length I decided that this must
end one way or the other, for good or for evil, and
I rode to her home to crave an answer to my suit.

The groom who took my horse directed me toward the garden, where, amid the formal flowerbeds
and flagstone paths, I found Lady Alice seated on
a carved bench in the shade of a clipped yew tree.
For a wonder, none of her many suitors was at hand,

but she was ever tender with children, and her young brother and sister now leaned against her knees as she read to them from a horn-book the tale of the Red Bull of Norroway. Either the warm sun or the story was too much for the children, who dozed gently, the little girl's Bartholomew baby upside down under her arm, the boy's popgun slipping from his relaxed hand. In a nearby fountain two stately swans paddled slowly about, bending their proud necks from time to time to admire their reflections in the water; and on the lawn there moved a flock of doves, searching for food and cooing gently as they searched.

It was a charming picture, and I halted to admire it, but Lady Alice saw me and beckoned me on, smiling and nodding, then laying finger to her lips and pointing to the sleeping children as I stepped across the turf. I understood, and in silence sat myself down on the grass before her, while she read on in a voice intentionally softened and monotonous. Beneath the hem of her satin gown I could see a hand's breadth of well-turned ankle enclosed in a silver-clocked stocking, and with some embarrassment I averted my eyes, lest she catch me looking and think me rude and over-bold. I would have been well content to sit for hours and listen to her sweet voice, to gaze on her fair cheeks that out-vied the peach in bloom, having no need of witchcraft or beauty secrets "to cleanse the blood and purify the skin," as old wives put it, who sell such charms; but the sun-dial had not marked a quarter of an hour when the wicket-gate clicked and another visitor crossed the lawn.

Looking up, I thought the dial must veil its face or belie the motto carven thereon—Non Numero Nisi Horas Serenas *—for the new-comer was the man I hated above all other, of whom I was most bitterly jealous, though policy and courtesy both forced me to conceal my hate.

Don Diego de Espinosa was a Spanish grandee who had come over in the train of Philip of Spain, when this latter came to marry our English Queen Mary. Some ten years older than myself, tall, athletic, darkly handsome, carrying himself with an air of distinction, courtly of manner, and deeply bitten with a fierce Castilian pride, he was a rival to be shunned, whether in love or in war. Not that I feared him, to be sure, so far as might regard any possible passage of arms, but I had good reason to be jealous, for his manner carried him far with the ladies, and he and I were the most in favor of all Lady Alice's suitors, nor might any tell on which she looked with greater pleasure. Beyond this, I distrusted the man, finding a hint of something sly and treacherous about his eyes, of cruelty about his

*I Number Only the Pleasant Hours.

33

lips. But of this I might not speak aloud, lest I seem to decry a rival. And there is no doubt that he worshipped Alice Chauntrey with a passion fully equal to my own.

Looking up, Lady Alice saw him, and with a slight grimace she moved, rousing the sleeping children.

"Alackaday, my dears!" she said. "Now must we be formal." And as they raised their tousled heads and rubbed their eyes I thrilled to be thus admitted to her intimacy.

Rising, she greeted Don Diego with grave courtesy, and perforce I did likewise.

"Speak to these gentlemen," Lady Alice told the children. "Then run and play. More of the Red Bull anon. Where is thy battledore, James? I will wager a groat on Marjorie."

Obedient, the children saluted us, then went to a remote corner of the lawn, while Don Diego and I seated ourselves on the bench, at a respectful distance from Lady Alice.

"What news from the court?" she asked us, lightly. "Or from the great city? How of this new tragedy of *Apius and Virginia?* Was it presented at court, as I hear was planned? And how did Her Most Gracious Majesty receive it? Was she pleased? I must persuade my father to take me for a visit to the city; alas, we grow most rustic

34

in this retirement!" She was evidently talking in some agitation, to forestall questions or perhaps to avert a quarrel which she may have thought imminent.

For a time we chatted of indifferent matters—Don Diego spoke English excellently well, though with a slight foreign accent—then rather abruptly he changed the course of our talk.

"Lady Alice," he said, "I would speak of a matter bearing some weight—"

"Nay, let us not be serious, this lovely day," she exclaimed, springing up. "See, I will challenge you to a game of battledore—Sir Richard and I against you, or you and I against him. Or will you help me give the pigeons their grain? Poor things! They have not been fed all day; see how diligently they seek for grubs upon the lawn! Do you not think grubs but a sorry diet? Of a surety, they would not please me!"

But Don Diego restrained her, though politely.

"This is a matter that must be spoken," he insisted. "I beg you, Lady Alice—"

"And how if I will not hear it?" she demanded, imperiously. "Will you force me to listen, willy-nilly?"

"Not so, indeed. But of your courtesy, I crave your attention." She paused, irresolute, and he went on: "Pray be seated; I will take but little of your time."

"At your command, my Lord." And she sat down again, folding her hands in her lap and composing her face to so demure a look that I was hard put to it to keep from laughing. "Your most obedient servant, Don Diego. I am all attention, and agog for your Lordship's words of wisdom."

I saw Espinosa's dark cheek flush at this teasing, but he answered smoothly enough.

"For two years now," he pursued, "Sir Richard Ayresford and I have been your most devoted suitors, aspirants for the honor of your hand. Surely you have divined our purpose?"

The corners of her mouth twitched, and she answered, prim as a cat that will not steal cream:

"I cannot deny that at times I have flattered myself with some such thought."

"Even so. And I have spoken to your worshipful parents, who are graciously pleased to approve my suit. So at last the time has come when you must choose between Sir Richard and myself."

"Indeed?" This with raised eyebrows and up-tilted chin. "And why?"

Don Diego was so taken aback by this cool question that I could not forbear smiling, whereat he scowled venomously at me. But I gave back a blank and innocent stare, though inwardly I was well pleased to see him thus treading on slippery ground; his Castilian arrogance would serve him ill in this encounter.

"Why must I choose between you two?" Lady Alice went on. "What if my maiden heart is bestowed elsewhere? And what if I say no to both?"

Don Diego frowned.

"But you cannot honorably do that. You have encouraged us, led us on—"

"Sir!"

Confused, he stammered an apology.

"It is well," she acknowledged his words. "And I would have you understand, Don Diego de Espinosa, that I am very well able to look to my own honor, nor do I crave guidance from anyone in these matters. Beyond which, I have a father who is somewhat tender of his daughter's good repute, nor is he ever reluctant to maintain it."

"I did not mean . . . I intended no discourtesy . . . I am not altogether at home in your language . . ."

"Nay—" she flashed him a tantalizing smile "—nay, you speak English admirably. Assuredly you make yourself understood. Sir, your pardon is granted. Proceed."

"None the less," he persisted, "I beg that you will declare your choice. It is not the custom of my family to dance attendance on any woman—"

37

"Nor are you obliged to do so now." This, very haughtily. "The Holy Virgin forbid that I should hold any man prisoner against his will, as the nymph Calypso did Odysseus. I can very well spare your attentions, Don Diego, should you wish to bestow the favor of your smile elsewhere. The road lies open before you, sir, and you are as free as any untaught falcon."

"Am I to take that for your answer, then?" His voice was hot with scarcely restrained anger.

She thought for a moment, her face relaxing in a roguish smile, and an impish look came into her eyes.

"What says Sir Richard?" she inquired. "Do you agree with Don Diego?"

It seemed that here was a chance to have my doubts resolved, and I replied, gravely:

"I would never have forced the choice, Lady Alice. But since Don Diego has seen fit to do so, I must admit that it seems no more than just."

"You tempt me strongly, gentlemen, to bid the grooms show you both the gate . . . but I will be merciful—oh, exceeding merciful! Not for me the cruelty of Dian, who caused her lover to be torn by hounds . . . well, let me think . . ." She tapped her teeth meditatively with a fingernail, then of a sudden broke into April smiles. "I will set you a test, like unto those Sir Thomas Malorie relates, in his goodly history of King Arthur and the Table Round. This, then, is my judgment. The Knights Hospitallers of St. John of Jerusalem, as you know, wage perpetual warfare against the followers of the black Mahound. Join that Order, fight for one year in aid of the Knights, and which of you bears himself with most distinction, him will I wed."

"But . . . but . . ." stammered Don Diego. "That is a celibate order, and to join it we must take a solemn vow never to marry. Surely you jest, Lady Alice!"

"Not a whit," she rejoined. "You need not take the full vows; join as Associates of the Order, for the term of a year and a day. That is permitted by their rules, and in such cases they will waive the period of probation."

"Further," pursued Espinosa, "they will not receive an aspirant unless he makes over to them a notable portion of his estates."

"Well, sir—" and she drew herself up proudly "—am I not worth some measures of land, some store of gold?"

"By St. Iago, yes! Lady Alice, I accept your challenge. And you, Sir Richard?"

"One thing occurs to me in opposition," I answered, slowly. "The Castilian langue of the Knights of St. John still exists, but the English langue was abolished by the father of our most gracious queen. And I understand that one of the conditions for membership is that the postulant must reside within the bounds of a Priory of the Order. Thus, I cannot see how I may join the Brotherhood."

"That need not hinder," explained Don Diego. "The langue of Castile will be glad to receive you, Sir Richard. Or, better yet, we will journey together to Paris, where both can join the langue of France. Even now the Knights are gathering their forces for an extraordinary effort against the Paynim, and at such a time they will not inquire too closely into your place of residence. Do you accept?"

"I do," was my reply, and we clasped hands on the agreement.

Then Lady Alice gave us her hands to kiss, and we took our leave, she bidding us godspeed and, like some damsel of the age of chivalry, bestowing on each a glove in token of her favor. To me she gave the left, sending me into transports of delight by a roguish whisper in my ear:

"The left hand is nearest the heart, Sir Richard."

"Also," I replied, in like tone, "that on which the wedding ring is worn." Whereat she blushed rosy red.

To be brief, Don Diego and I journeyed together to the Commandery of Paris, for I might not avoid his company without grave discourtesy. There, hav-

ing proved our sixteen quarterings of nobility and
made out the papers assigning to the Hospitallers
a goodly share of our estates, we were tested, in-
structed, and accepted as Associates of the Order,
with all the duties of the Knights of Justice save that
we took no vow of eternal celibacy, and all the
privileges save that of voting for the officers. Jehan
de Rohan and Sir Oliver Starkey stood my sponsors,
while Don Diego was sponsored by two other
Knights, the Chevalier de Medrano and Don Alvaro
de Sandé. Passage was taken for us on a caravel
bound for the chef lieu of the Knights, the island
of Malta, but, as I have related, we were driven
by a storm upon the coast of Spain.

All this I told my comrades in arms as we sat
under the canopy of the Grand Master's galley,
and many a laugh or exclamation vouchsafed their
interest, changing to oaths and bitter curses when
I related my treatment at the hands of the Holy
Office.

"By St. Denis of France!" broke out young la
Vallette, when I had finished. "It is like some tale
of Amadis of Gaul, or of Angelica and Orlando,
with the young knight going forth to battle in
honor of his lady. Is it not, Uncle?" For the
Grand Master had joined us in time to hear somewhat of the tale.

The elder la Vallette nodded, smiling his kindly smile.

"It would, perhaps, be better," he suggested, "did the knight go forth to war for the love of Our Blessed Redeemer, to uphold His kingdom against the foul Paynim, rather than for a carnal love."

"We have in our country a proverb," laughed de la Mara, "which says: 'When they bring thee a heifer, make haste with the halter.' For my part, I am content to have a good sword on my side, whatever his reason for fighting. And by the Hand of St. John, if Sir Richard fights like his countryman, Sir Oliver, here, I will extend my heartiest thanks to the Dona Alice Chauntrey!"

"And in England we have also a proverb," Sir Oliver Starkey offered, " 'Look not a gift horse in the mouth.' I am content that Sir Richard is with us, whatever the cause."

It was wonderful to me to see the freedom which the Knights used toward their leader. Knowing his dignity and his exalted position, equal to those of any crowned head, I had thought that the Grand Master must of necessity be austere and unapproachable, but this was far from the case; they were all friends together, and la Vallette was their chief— our chief—solely because he had the strongest character, the wisest brain. He could be stern and severe when occasion required, as I saw later, and as, in truth, I had seen in the torture-chamber, but thus early in our acquaintance I learned a lesson never to be forgotten—that the man who deserves respect need never ask it.

"Well, well," said la Vallette, "we will not question Sir Richard's motives. And there is no denying that he comes at a most opportune time."

This last was explained to me by de la Mara, for our mutual liking ripened quickly to an affection which was to last for many years. Being by chance together at the galley's prow, with no others at hand, I asked Juan to tell me something of the Knights and of their home.

"I know, of course," I said, "that the Order numbers the best blood of the world, that it is exceeding rich and powerful—I saw its power manifested in Barcelona!—and that it was founded for the relief of human suffering, to aid the wounded and diseased, whatever their station. Also, that it has Commanderies throughout all Europe, and that it is divided into seven languages, or nations, those of Italy, Aragon, Castile, France, Auvergne, Provence, and Germany. But beyond this, little. My acceptance was somewhat hasty, and my preceptors laid stress on the duties of a Knight rather than on the history of the Order."

"There was reason for this haste, as you will understand, friend Ricardo—I may so call you?"

"I shall be honored."

"And let me add that my sponsors in baptism gave me the name of Juan, for the use and ease of my friends. Well, then, without abating its purpose of aid and comfort to the distressed, the Order has, with the passage of years, somewhat extended its functions. As perchance you do not know, the Knights Hospitallers have been a thorn in the side of Islam since the founding of the Order, five hundred years agone. We have fought the Moslem on land and sea, our galleys harry his coasts, and more than any other we have withstood his planned invasion of Christendom. Driven successively from Jerusalem, from Acre, and from Cyprus by the whole weight of the Ottoman Empire, we took refuge in the island of Rhodes, whence also we were driven, to wander for seven years, like Æneas, about the Mediterranean. All this, of course, was before my time, you understand."

"Surely, I understand."

"At length, in the year 1530 of Our Blessed Redeemer, the heroic de l'Isle Adam, being then Grand Master, led the Knights to Malta, which was granted them by a charter of the Emperor Charles, father to the present king of Spain. The island was well-nigh a barren rock, but with shiploads of earth from Sicily and the mainland ground was made, and crops and flowers planted, till now it outdoes in beauty the Isle of Roses,* whence we came. Also, the quarries of the island furnished rocks for strong and noble fortifications.

"From Malta our galleys have swept over the sea, carrying death and destruction to the Moslem towns of Africa and sinking the corsairs of the Barbary Coast, wherever found. Angered at this, the sultan, Solyman the Sublime, as he arrogantly calls himself, has vowed to drive us from our present home even as he drove us from Rhodes, and to that end is preparing an armada against us. Learning the sultan's intent from spies and deserters, the Grand Master is calling in all who can be spared from the Commanderies of Europe, is laying in stores of provisions and arms, and, in brief, is making ready for a siege. There is no doubt that it will be a bitter one, for the sultan is raging against us, even as a wild beast, and we, on our part, are vowed to let no Moslem make good a footing on our island. Beyond question, many of us will die, but how could one die better than in defending the cross of Christ against the base followers of Mahound? Eh, amigo de mi corazón—friend of my heart? Is it not a glorious death that lies before us?"

"For myself," I answered, dryly, "I should prefer a glorious victory. Let the Turks enjoy the glorious death."

* Rhodes.

45

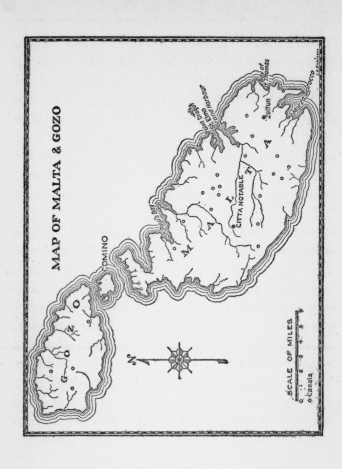

MAP OF MALTA & GOZO

GOZO

COMINO

St. Paul's Bay

MALTA

San Diesu
St. Elmo
Grand Harbour

CITTA NOTABLE

Zeitun

Bay of
St. Thomas

Marsasirocco

N.

SCALE OF MILES
0   1   2   3   4   5   6

o Casals

He stared for a moment, then burst out laughing and slapped me on the shoulder.

"You fish-blooded English!" he said. "Cold, austere—and yet most marvellous fighters! How do you do it? I am not of the hot south—my home is the cold province of Aragon—yet I am fiery beside you or Sir Oliver."

"We are slow to rouse," I told him. "But we are like that tortoise of the Western Seas, of which I have heard travelers speak, which having once taken hold with its jaws does not let go until it hears the thunder."

He laughed again.

"A merry conceit, that! Yet with no small measure of truth, as touches the English. Well, you are like to hear thunder in plenty, once the siege begins, though it will be the thunder of the Moslem guns."

"Tell me something of the island," I begged. "I have never been there, nor have I heard it described."

"It is not easy to draw a picture with words, and you will soon see it for yourself. However, if you wish. . . . It is, then, some seventeen miles long by half as broad, lying northwest and southeast, with the isle of Gozo, half its size, to the north, and separated from Malta by a channel some two miles in width. Gozo has a small castle, but little else of

47

interest, for which reason refractory or disobedient Knights are sometimes punished by a longer or shorter exile there. Our island is rough and rocky, with hills rising six or seven hundred feet above the sea, and with numerous wretched casals, or villages, scattered about its surface. Near the center is a city which the natives call Città Notable, though it is but a poor thing to one who has seen Rome or Madrid—or, I make no doubt, London," he added, in courtesy.

"The chief harbor, where we have our home, is on the northeastern coast, and is a noble one, two miles in length by one in breadth. A point of land extends down the middle, like a tongue in an open mouth, and is crowned by Mount Sceberras; Fort St. Elmo, one of our strong places, lies on the tip of the tongue. North of the promontory is Marza Muscetto Harbor, and south of it the Grand Harbor. On the south—rather, the southeastern—shore of the Grand Harbor are five promontories, which might be likened to the creature's teeth, with bays between them, and on the end of the third of these is Fort St. Angelo, with the town of Il Borgo behind it, on the landward side. It is here that the Order has its home, the Knights dwelling in the castle, the islanders in the town. There are a few noble buildings in Il Borgo, for the island boasts some families of gentle blood, though by a rule of

48

the Order no Maltese can become one of the
Knights of St. John. On the fourth tooth, near the
base, is Fort St. Michael, with a handful of miser-
able dwellings clustering about its foot. Oh, we
are well equipped to bite, as the Moslem shall learn,
for our fortifications are as stout as any in all
Christendom."

"How of the people?" I asked. "The natives."

"Good folk," Juan replied, with enthusiasm.
"Sound folk. Pleasant and friendly, if a thought
quick in the temper. The men admirable fighters,
the women in the main beautiful, with their small
hands and feet, their dainty yet well-rounded figures,
their black eyes and hair, olive skins, and full red
lips, most seductively kissable. To see one of those
piquant faces smiling at you from the shadow of
the great black hood, like an overgrown monk's
cowl, which they call the faldetta *—Sancta Maria,
it is to lose one's heart!"

"Tut, tut!" I grinned. "What talk is this for
one who has taken a vow of lifelong celibacy, who
has sworn to kiss no woman, not even a sister, and
to hold no child over the font of baptism?"

"Nay," he rejoined, eagerly, "I have taken no

---

* Some writers on Malta say that the faldetta was adopted
in 1798 as a sign of mourning for the French occupation of the
island, but it is certainly older than this, being mentioned in records
of the Order prior to that date. The exact time of its introduction
is uncertain.

vow of celibacy; I am an Associate of the Order,
like yourself, not a Knight of Justice. And though
I am no libertine, nor have a roving eye, such vows
as I have sworn have not destroyed my sense of
feminine beauty. Still," he admitted, "it were perhaps as well that the Grand Master should not hear
me speak thus; he would exile me to Gozo, or sen-
tence me to eat my meals from the floor for a
month. Our leader is a wonderful man, in truth,
but he has little sympathy with female charms—the
sole flaw in a character of the finest," he mourned,
only half in jest.

"Whence came the folk of Malta? Have they
always held the island?"

Juan shrugged.

"Who knows? Some say they are of Greek de-
scent; that Gozo is Ogygia, Calypso's isle, where
Odysseus tarried in his wanderings, and this may
be true; certes it is pleasant and fertile enough to
be the home of a goddess. Some believe that the
folk are of ancient Tyre, whence Dido fled. This
gains color from certain images of stone which were
found in the quarries; squat, seated figures with nodding heads, which Brother Robert, who is learned in
such matters, declared to be idols of Astarte, the
moon-goddess of Phœnicia. Still others hold that the
folk are of Italy, Christians who fled from the perse-
cutions of Nero; and we know that the holy St. Paul

was wrecked there while journeying from Cæsarea to Rome; the bay where he was cast ashore still bears his name. And indeed there are vast catacombs, like those of Rome, hewn in the living rock. If opportunity offers, we will explore these passages together, you and I. Their extent you may judge when I tell you that Ras Hanzier, the Promontory of the Sow, near the western end of the Grand Harbor, takes its name from one of those animals which, having been lost underground in Città Notable, came out on the shore five miles from where it disappeared."

"I can see," I commented, "that there is much of interest to be found there, aside from the efforts of Solyman the Sublime."

"And I predict," Juan answered, "that you will lose your heart to some black-eyed Paula or Francesca or Carmela. Nay"—as I shook my head— "not of the common folk; I would not insult you, Ricardo mio. But there is good blood on the island; be sure of that. More than one family can show its quarterings of nobility, and there is more than one honored name there."

But I smiled and shook my head again; my heart was safe in the keeping of a blue-eyed damsel of England, and the dark maidens of the south held no charm for me.

A favoring wind springing up, the mariners spread

our three huge lateen sails, thus greatly augmenting our speed, and the voyage was soon over—too soon for me, who enjoyed every moment of it, being exempt from the horrible sickness of the sea which overtook some of our party. In general, the Knights were a pleasant, friendly group, each one a courtly, high-bred gentleman, and though they took their duties seriously, they were in no degree pompous or cold. They had relaxed somewhat from the austere Rule of Raymond, as originally laid down for their guidance, and though they practiced moderation and continence in all things, I believe this was more due to a feeling that licence did not become a gentleman than from any monkish tendencies. At all events, they were delightful companions, and took me freely into their number, so that, although eager to see my new home, I could have wished the journey longer than it was.

But at length we came in sight of the island, and some hours later turned its southern coast, with the overseers marching up and down the runways and plying the lash with renewed vigor on the backs of our naked oarsmen. Thus urged, the slaves— all captive Moslems—made the stout ash oars creak and bend, driving us at speed over the incredibly blue water. And as we rounded into the harbor the lookouts on shore recognized the Grand Master's pennon at our masthead, and from St. Elmo on our

right and from the towering masses of St. Angelo
and St. Michael on our left, guns boomed salute and
flags waved joyous welcome.

Busy days followed for us all. Under direction
of Girolamo Cassar, an Italian who was la Vallette's own engineer and architect, gangs of men
labored to quarry rock, drag it to the strongholds,
and further strengthen the strong fortifications. It
seemed to me that these were already impregnable,
but Cassar laughed at me when I said as much.

"Nay, Sir Richard," he replied, "it is plain that
you have had but little experience of war. Wait till
you see the artillery and breaching-pieces the Turks
will bring against us. No mere falconets or sakers
—though in truth there will be plenty of those—
but huge basilicas hurling marble bullets heavier
than a man." I must have looked my doubt, for
he added: "Nay, I lie not. When Byzantium fell,
Mahomet had in use great guns whose bullets weighed
as much as four men, though I question if they will
bring such giant pieces against us, these being over-
heavy to come by sea. But we cannot build our walls
too strong."

So all that winter we toiled to make ourselves
secure. I was given command of a gang of men
in one of the quarries of Gozo, and dwelt in a tent
on that island, returning to St. Angelo, where were
the Grand Master and most of the Knights, only for

the Sabbath or to hear Mass on some special saint's day. Of necessity, I learned the Maltese tongue, and found my workmen all that de la Mara had said; loyal, steady, in the main good-natured, and somewhat quick in the temper. I had no trouble with them, beyond having to separate two who fell to carving each other with knives, and when the winter was spent our showing had been so good that the Grand Master was pleased to commend me. I passed this commendation on to my men, which seemed to hearten them no little.

Vessels came in from time to time, bringing reinforcements from all Europe, and when spring arrived we mustered altogether, for the defence of the island, between five and six hundred Knights and twelve hundred mercenary soldiers—mostly Italian—as well as seven thousand Maltese volunteers. Altogether, men, women, and children, there were some twenty-five thousand souls on Malta and seven or eight thousand on Gozo.

The galley-slaves, to the number of five hundred, were confined in caves dug in the rock of the Port of Galleys, where they lived when not at their oars. They were allowed to bathe in a small bay of the port, known as the Bay of Vermin, though I cannot say whether this was a contemptuous name for the slaves themselves or alluded to the parasites with which they were infested; in any case, they were a filthy lot. In May, la Vallette issued a proclamation to these slaves, promising them freedom if they would aid the Knights faithfully during the siege, and though it seemed to me strange to offer them a choice between slavery and warring against their own countrymen, I must admit that it turned out well; many of them exhibited the odd spectacle of Moslems fighting stoutly for Christ, and these were duly rewarded—such of them as survived.

Many bastions had been constructed, that of Castile being on the landward side of Il Borgo, while others were on the promontory of la Sangle, where stood St. Michael's fort, and on the point beneath St. Angelo. Each of the principal points of defence was given in charge of one or another of the langues, that our spirits might be fired by knightly emulation. I might say here that this division into langues, though originally of some significance, had with the passing of years come to mean but little; a man might belong to that of the country where he was accepted, or to that of his friends. Thus, I was of the French langue, having been accepted at Paris, whereas Sir Oliver Starkey, though English born like myself, was of that of Provence, since the Grand Master, whose secretary and firm friend he was, was Provençal.

It was considered that St. Elmo would be the first point of attack, since its thirty guns commanded the

Grand Harbor, and about eight hundred men, mostly volunteers, were stationed here. The fort was well enough defended on its seaward side by the waters of the Mediterranean, and on the landward was built up and protected by a dry ditch, a counterscarp, and a ravelin. The command was entrusted to an aged Knight of the Italian langue, named de Broglio, and to reinforce him la Vallette sent sixty Knights under a most able veteran of many wars, the Bailiff of Negropont. Also, two companies of foreign mercenaries under the Chevalier de la Cerda were added to the garrison, thus completely filling the fort's accommodations. Unfortunately, the magazines would not hold any great store of supplies, so St. Elmo must depend for food and ammunition on Il Borgo, across the water. This was a cause of much anxiety to la Vallette, who foresaw that if the Turks had wit enough to cut off communication between the two, St. Elmo must quickly fall. However, there was naught to be done about it save commend ourselves to God and hope that the holy St. John would blind the Paynim's eyes.

For myself, I was now stationed in St. Angelo, helping to direct the work of strengthening the defences of Il Borgo and razing many outlying buildings where the enemy could find lodgement. About a thousand Moslem slaves, taken from the prisons and chained together in couples, were chiefly used for this work, and we drove them hard under the lash, till at times I almost felt some measure of pity for the wretches. But when such feelings stirred in me I had but to think of the coast towns of Italy and France and Spain—yes, even of England—ravaged by these vile creatures; of the men and boys slain or torn from their homes to toil under the Afric sun or guard the harems of Tunis and Algiers; of the women and girls outraged and dragged to a captivity worse than death, to satisfy the lust of some base lascivious worshipper of Mahound; and my heart grew hard again. Surely God Himself could not pity these human fiends!

My tasks were not so pressing but that I had some leisure time, and thus I came to know the Church of St. Lawrence, where were kept the sacred relics, including the trumpet which signalled the withdrawal from Rhodes; the miraculous image of Our Lady of Philermo; the figurehead of the ship in which de l'Isle Adam came to Malta; the mummied hand of the holy St. John, presented to the Order by the sultan Bajazet; and most wonderful of all, and most worthy our adoration, an undoubted fragment of the True Cross. Also, Juan and I spent many hours exploring the catacombs, which held a peculiar fascination for him, and these explorations were destined to be of great service to the Order after the siege began.

Among the recruits brought by vessels from the mainland was, to my no small disgust, Don Diego de Espinosa. I had not mourned his loss, and if the truth were told, though I would not wish him harm, it was in the nature of a disappointment to find him alive and well. He gave me a courteous greeting which I am sure it hurt him to extend, and hiding my feelings I returned it in kind. It seems— or so he said—that he had taken a pleurisy of the chest from exposure during the wreck, and lay ill for months in Barcelona. On hearing of my adventures:

"It grieves me," he remarked, "that I did not know of your peril. I have some small influence, and might have been of assistance to you. At the worst, I could have testified in your behalf."

"I had no means of informing you," I rejoined. "Nay, I did not even know that you still lived."

"True, true. Well, I am glad that matters turned out so fortunately. It is not everyone who has the good luck to escape, having once fallen into the hands of the Holy Office. My congratulations, Sir Richard."

"It was not wholly a matter of luck," I answered, dryly, to which he agreed:

"Faith, no! Still, I am glad to felicitate you."

And bidding us a polite farewell, he went his way.

I say "us," for de la Mara was with me at the time, and he cocked a humorous eye after Don Diego.

"If he was glad to hear of your escape," said Juan, "may I never again taste the Blessed Sacrament! Ricardo mio, I would not trust him too far; he has a slinky look." And he made the sign of the horns, to ward off the evil eye.

"I do not trust him at all," I answered, shortly, and Juan laughed.

"I see you know your way about," he chuckled. "Well, let the hen live, though it have the pip. Now, touching this loan of a few slaves, to mount my guns—"

At length, on the eighteenth day of May, in the year 1565 of Our Blessed Redeemer, from the ramparts of St. Elmo, St. Angelo, and St. Michael boomed the signal guns which told the approach of the long-awaited Turkish fleet, and warned the country folk to withdraw into their villages. All of us who might do so hastened to the ramparts or other point of vantage to watch the foe as they came on, a hundred and eighty great galleys, with many transports, all with sails drawing, oars flashing, banners flying, and decks crowded with men eager for the adventure, for what they deemed a holy war.

Sir Oliver Starkey was standing in a group of

Knights on the ramparts of St. Angelo, and gazing at the invaders through a curious instrument given him by an Italian alchemist, a friend of the Grand Master, one Giambattista della Porta, who had made this so-called "optic glass." It was a metal tube something less than an ell in length, with curved pieces of glass fixed at the ends, and possessed the strange power of making distant objects seem near at hand. Several times during the siege I had the opportunity of looking through it, and can vouch for its miraculous power.

"Not less than thirty thousand men," reported Sir Oliver. "I can see the horsetail standards, and the banners of Pialé the admiral, and of Mustapha Pasha. Also the gold broidered white silk banners of the Yeni-Tscheri.* Pardi, it is great honor that Solyman does us—he is sending against us the very flower of the Ottoman Empire! Well, we should have much pleasurable fighting ere the siege comes to an end."

And now, as the leading Moslem galleys swept around the southeastern point of the island to anchor in Marza Scirocco, there was unfurled above us the Banner of St. John, with its eight-pointed cross of white; and our sweet-toned trumpets blew defiance at the foe. Back from the Moslems came the sound

* Commonly called Janizaries. The choicest troops of the Turkish army, drafted of Christian children and rigorously trained.

of trumpet and naker and cymbal, and from the admiral's galley a single gun boomed its challenge.

The bells of St. Lawrence called us to the church, and as we took our places, the Grand Master appeared before us. He had changed his black cloak of peace for the scarlet surcoat of war, with the white cross of St. John on back and breast, and his noble head was thrown proudly back as he surveyed our ranks.

"Knights of St. John," his deep voice rang out, "there lies the foe against whom we are vowed to eternal warfare. To-morrow he comes against us with sword and flame. Join me now in commending ourselves to God, Whose faithful servants we are." We knelt on the stones, and with la Vallette leading us we repeated in unison the Paternoster, the Ave, and the Credo, together with that noble psalm which begins: "Benedictus Dominus Deus meus, Qui docet manus meas ad prœlium et digitos meos ad bellum."

"To your quarters now," the Grand Master went on, "and prepare for the fray, that we may acquit ourselves like men and that we may do our utmost devoir in this stern fight against the infidel, the Antichrist, to the greater glory of Our Father in Heaven and for the patron saint of our Order, the blessed St. John, whose holy name we bear."

CHAPTER III

Of the Poisoned Spring; and the Lady
Madeleine d'Armagnac

ON the morning after the Turkish fleet arrived, the Grand Master sent for me. I found him in his quarters in the castle of St. Angelo, and both he and Sir Oliver greeted me pleasantly, la Vallette plunging directly into the matter for which I was summoned.

"Sir Richard," he began, "I have a task for you. Sufficiently ungrateful, I fear, but necessary."

"I am vowed to obedience," I replied, and he acknowledged the words by a nod.

"Briefly," he continued, "it is thus. There is no doubt that the invaders will first attack St. Elmo, since while that stands their galleys cannot force the passage of the Grand Harbor, to come at St. Michael and St. Angelo from the water-front. To do this they will unquestionably open lines at the foot of Mount Sceberras, and also plant men and guns on the promontory at the mouth of Marza Muscetto. And since the men must have water, they will get it from the spring of Sliema. You know where that is?"

"Perfectly, yes."

"Good! Now, an Italian friend of the Order, having made some researches into the wisdom of the Medicis and the Borgias, has given me a store of most deadly poison for such use, and this I would have you place in the spring."

He spoke the simple truth when he called the task ungrateful. Of all base, unknightly deeds—to poison a foe's drinking water! My disgust showed on my face, I think, for la Vallette went on:

"You must not take this in the usual light, Sir Richard. It is not as though we were knavishly destroying an honorable foe. These invaders are the enemies of Christ, ravishers of women, vile beyond all words—foul vermin, whom to destroy by any means whatever is acceptable in the sight of God. His Holiness of Rome has given his blessing to our defence of the island, approving in advance whatever we may do. No, you must not think of it with abhorrence, but as a needful, though perchance unpleasant, task."

There was no help for it; I liked the assignment not at all, but it must be done. So I merely bowed and asked:

"When do I go?"

"To-night, under cover of darkness. You had best set out shortly after vespers, perhaps, though I leave that to your judgment; you will choose your own

63

time. The poison is in four earthen jars of about a stone weight each. Select what companions you need, with men to carry the jars. And God speed you!"

"May I take the Chevalier de la Mara?"

"Yes, certainly. Sir Oliver, will you indite an order to that effect?" Sir Oliver did so, handing the parchment to me. "The poison will be delivered at your quarters before dusk," la Vallette concluded. "It is vastly potent, so use care in the handling of it." And he dismissed me.

With the order, I went in search of Juan, who swore mightily when he learned our errand.

"Sancta Maria, is it the act of a friend, Ricardo," he reproached me, "to involve me in so shameful a deed?"

I shrugged my shoulders, finding myself in the position of defending an act I could not like.

"Consider two things," I answered. "First, we have complete absolution—"

"That does not make it less unknightly!"

"Perchance. But it may ease our consciences somewhat. And second, what we do to-night may quite well be the means of saving some of our brethren."

"True," he admitted, after some reflection. "True. And in that light, I am with you. After all, what matter whether we slay the vermin with steel

64

or poison? Whether the stone hits the pitcher or
the pitcher the stone, it goes ill with the pitcher."

We made our plans and arrangements, choosing
four men to go with us. One of them, Hamilcar
Xuereb, a Maltese, had been headman of my gang
in the quarry, and another, David Evans, was pilot
of the transport which had taken the stone from
Gozo to the Grand Harbor. Thus I knew them
both well, and knew them to be stout of heart and
strong of arm; Xuereb, in particular, was of Her-
culean build and very quick in his motions, an excellent man in a fight. He wore great drooping black
moustachios which, with his swarthy skin and dark
eyes, made him appear the very archetype of a Sicilian bandit, though he was in truth the best-natured
and gentlest man who ever sent a Moslem soul yowl-
ing to Gehenna fires. Though ferocious against the
infidel, he was vastly kind with women, and in time
of peace had usually a crowd of children, his own
and others, about him.

Evans was English born, though his forefathers
were of Wales, and he inherited their love of battle,
their venturesome spirit. A short, stocky man he
was, bandy-legged almost to deformity, with the
rolling gait all sailors have, and icy cool in battle—
naught ever shook his nerves. In imitation of some
admiral or other under whom he had served, he wore
his fiery red beard trimmed to a point, and his mous-

tachios neatly waxed. For the rest, he had large brown eyes, was not unhandsome, and spoke ever in a coldly cynical fashion that belied the fires within.

The other two were nothing notable; merely good Spanish soldiers whom Juan selected from among his men at the bastion. Assembling the four, we outlined the task, cautioned them against speaking of it, and relieved them from duty, that they might rest and be fresh for the night's labors.

Juan and I then mounted to the highest point of St. Angelo's battlements, to gaze abroad and learn what we could of the foe's dispositions. There was little to be seen, however. The main point of interest lay in two galleys which we watched making their way across the mouth of the Grand Harbor toward the promontory beyond Marza Muscetto. They were laden with artillery and crowded with men, and we conjectured that Mustapha was planning to establish a battery on that spur of land, even as la Vallette had predicted.

Presently a group of gaily clad horsemen came riding over the hill and down toward Il Borgo. We lost sight of them in the streets of the town, but shortly heard the notes of a horn blown at the castle gate.

"An embassy from the Moslems, beyond a doubt," said Juan. "Shall we go listen to their message, and to the Grand Master's reply?"

I agreed, and we descended to the audience chamber of the castle, where we found la Vallette seated in state, a hundred or so of the Knights grouped about him. The embassy, half a dozen in number, were admitted soon after Juan and I took our places, and I gazed at them with interest, for they were the only Turks I had ever seen close at hand. I took in their flowing garments, their turbans, their curved scimitars, and I realized that they were men of rank, for they bore themselves proudly and their clothing and weapons were literally sown with gems. And I must admit that their features surprised me, for I had been led to believe that the Moslems were demons, fiends of the Pit, but these were fine-looking warriors, with their thin, high-arched noses, bold black eyes, and prideful mien. I whispered as much to Juan, and he replied:

"These are their noblemen, their men of quarterings; the common herd are vastly other. Besides," he added, succinctly, "handsome is that handsome does." That man had a proverb for every occasion of life!

With many genuflections and much show of courtesy, the ambassadors approached the Grand Master, when, receiving permission, the chief addressed to la Vallette a lengthy speech, of which I understood only the words "Solyman," "Mustapha," and "la Vallette," for it was in the Turkish language. The Grand Master, however, had in his youth been for some time a prisoner among the Turks, and spoke their tongue fluently, as did most of the Knights, who now listened with attention. Juan gave me a summary of the speech.

"After reciting the sultan's titles, as well as those of the Grand Master, he called on la Vallette to surrender the island, and promised us honorable terms; or if we are obdurate, death to the Knights, slavery to the commoners, and devastation to Malta —hush! La Vallette is about to speak."

Rising, the Grand Master replied briefly, though in a courteous manner, but a roar of laughter burst from the Knights, and they clapped one another on the back in delight.

"What said he?" I whispered to Juan, who controlled his mirth long enough to answer:

"He thanked Mustapha for his kind offer, but said that God would uphold the right. Then he added: 'Tell your master that there are many who come for wool but go back shorn.' Ho, by the Hand of St. John, God send that the jest prove truth!"

The ambassadors were rewarded with princely gifts and dismissed, and Juan and I betook ourselves to rest, for the afternoon was drawing on.

At dusk we were roused, went to offer prayers in the Church of St. Lawrence, ate, and made ready for our expedition. Our men reported to us at the appointed time, and with Juan and myself leading and the others carrying the jars of poison, we set out.

The journey was about five miles by land, but we judged that safer than going by water, for the Turks had not yet established themselves to north of us, but might not impossibly be guarding Muscetto Harbor. So we decided to follow along the shore, which we could do without exceeding difficulty, for though the coast was rugged, the moon was full, enabling us to avoid obstacles. The trip was utterly uneventful, and we reached our destination some time before midnight, finding that the dry weather of the past weeks had caused the spring to be rather lower than usual.

"That is well," said Juan. "The water being below the outfall, our poison will not be carried off and wasted."

The men emptied the fine white powder into the spring and stirred the water until the poison was all dissolved. Our task done, we were about to retire, when we heard men approaching, talking as they came. We could not tell how many there might be, and had we fled the moonlight would have discovered us, so I bade my men take shelter behind the boulders which lay thick-sown all about.

Crouching in the shadows, we saw a score of Turks draw near, each carrying two great earthen jars slung from a pole across his shoulders, and these

jars they filled, jabbering the while in their outland-
ish tongue. When they had got the water and
departed, I called my party together, finding Juan
greatly excited.

"Did you hear what they were saying, Ricardo?"
he asked, eagerly. "Did you? Nay, I forgot—you
do not know their language."

"I heard it," spoke up the Englishman, Evans.
"God's curse on them!"

"Where did you learn their speech?" inquired
Juan, with some curiosity.

"While a prisoner among them," Evans returned.
"Two years I spent among the Paynim hounds."

"And how did you escape?"

"Oh, I turned Moslem," he replied, indifferently.

"What!" I cried, in horror. "You denied God?"

Evans had made a journey to the Brazil some
years before, and had there acquired the habit of
chewing the leaves of a certain Indian herb, whereof
he carried always a supply about him. He now
crammed a handful into his mouth, chewed for a
moment, and spat voluminously into the spring.

"Nay," he answered, "I said the Fatihah, the first
chapter of the Koran, which is their confession of
faith, much as the Credo is with us. But I kept my
right hand behind me as I did so, with the fore and
middle fingers crossed, that the good God might
know I meant it not. Having thus won my freedom,

I performed the hajj, or pilgrimage to Mecca, which is enjoined on all true believers in Islam. Thereby I gained the right to wear a green turban, together with much consideration from the followers of Mahound; and I obtained three slaves, a nice plump wife, and, more important than all else, a chance to escape."

I could not forbear laughing at the casual manner in which he related all this, but I said:

"It will go hard with you if you are retaken. They are bitter, I am told, against those who relapse, having once professed Islam."

"It will go harder yet with those who try to retake me. One such experience is ample; I am no hog, and know when I have had enough. Though I do wish," he added, thoughtfully, "that I could have brought my wife away with me. She was very beautiful, affectionate, and properly submissive—the only good thing about their accursed religion is the meekness it breeds in their women. She was far different from my English wife."

"Válgame Dios!" exclaimed Juan, amazed. "How many wives have you?"

Evans counted on his fingers.

"One in England, one among the Turks, one in the Brazil—a pretty little red girl, that one—one in Muscovy, when I was there with Master Richard Chanceler, some twelve years back. It was an expedition enterprised by Sir Hugh Willoughby, for whom Master Chanceler was major pilot. Sir Hugh was cast away and lost, but our vessel, by the grace of God, reached Muscovy, where is no night at all during the summer months, but a continual light, the sun never setting. There I took this woman, but she was flat-faced, greasy, dirty, and full of lice, so that I mourned not to leave her. My Turkish wife was inclined to be dirty, until I had beaten her for it some three or four times. Oh, yes, and two in France—six in all. And I am now betrothed to one in Il Borgo."

"Madre de Dios! I should think you were already sufficiently be-wived for any reasonable man. Small wonder that you were willing to turn Moslem, though you appear to have exceeded even their liberal bounds of marriage, which permit a man but four wives. Well, this is all very fine, but the question is, what is to be done?"

"Return to St. Angelo," I replied, promptly. "Our mission is accomplished."

"Nay, Ricardo mio, you do not understand. It was plain from the talk of these men that a Christian lady is being held prisoner by one of their officers, to be kept for his harem. Can we, as true gentlemen, permit this? Is it not necessary, for our honor, that we attempt her rescue?"

I considered this problem, then said:

"Granting it to be an outrage, still it might be thought rash for six men to attack the whole Turkish army. Do you know where to find her?"

"In the camp near St. Thomas' Bay, not far from the ruined temple of the Phœnicians."

"Not this side the Grand Harbor?"

"No."

"Then it is out of the question for to-night; we cannot reach St. Thomas' bay ere dawn. Come; we can talk this over to-morrow. Now for home."

We cast the poison-jars into the harbor some distance from the spring, and reached St. Angelo shortly before sunrise. Juan was still agitated with the thought of saving the Christian captive, and it was with difficulty that I could calm him and persuade him to sleep. For myself, I was as anxious as he to rescue the lady from that vile slavery, but it seemed beyond hope.

With morning, I reported to the Grand Master and received his approval, and I may say here that our mission was not without success, for we learned afterward, from prisoners, that more than eight hundred Turks died of the poison ere they abandoned the spring. Also, I told la Vallette of the captive lady, asking permission to attempt her rescue, but this he peremptorily refused.

"It is too dangerous an enterprise, Sir Richard," he said. "I feel for her, and were there an assur-

ance of success it might be tried, but I cannot spare
even one of my Knights; every sword will be needed.
I am sorry to damp your chivalry, but it may not
be." And with that I was obliged to content myself,
reporting as much to Juan, who was sorely grieved,
but acquiesced perforce.

The Turks had already begun to establish themselves on the island, and had raided a number of the
villages, including Città Notable. The damage was
slight, and the loss of life nothing, for the country
folk, gathering in Città Notable, took refuge in the
catacombs, where the Turks dared not follow for
fear of ambush. But la Vallette sent out a body of
cavalry under the Grand Marshal, the Chevalier
Coppier, to meet these raiders, though I think his
purpose was more than anything else to familiarize
us with the appearance and manner of fighting of the
Turks. Juan was on duty at the bastion of Castile,
but I went with the expedition, and enjoyed some
very sprightly encounters; the Turks were by no
means to be despised. However, we had good success, and sent a number of heads back to Il Borgo,
but at length, when two Knights and several commoners had been slain, the Grand Marshal ordered
a retirement.

We took half a dozen of prisoners back with us,
and these the Grand Master questioned closely, to
learn what he could of the foe's dispositions. When

he had finished, I craved permission to examine them.

"I would learn," I said, "if there is not some way in which the Christian lady may be rescued."

La Vallette smiled.

"Is that bee still buzzing in your casque, Sir Richard?" he inquired. "Well, take them. But remember, no rash act without direct leave."

I thanked him, then summoned a file of men, removed the captives to a dungeon, and sent one man for de la Mara and another for a charcoal brazier and some pointed irons, such as are used for destroying the eyes of prisoners. When Juan came, I told him what was in my mind, and he questioned the Turks; to my great relief the sight of the white-hot irons was enough, and we did not have to use persuasion. The men talked freely, glad to escape blinding and torture by telling all they knew, and at length Juan declared himself satisfied. I sent the prisoners off to the Port of Galleys, and de la Mara told me what they had said.

"The lady was taken, Ricardo, in a raid on the French coast; she is of France, it seems. She is the prisoner of a certain aga, or colonel, named Yussef, and is held in his tent, near the Bay of St. Thomas. They described his tent and his banner, so that I could recognize the place with ease. When do we go?"

"Softly, softly, Juan," I told him. "I will borrow
Sir Oliver's optic glass, and to-morrow we will make
a little reconnaisance, then lay our plans, if the matter seems in any way feasible."

"Oh, you cold-blooded English!" he mourned.
"But, by St. Iago, it must be feasible—we must make
it so! It does not become our manhood to let a
Christian lady be dragged to an Algerine harem.
We must, Ricardo—do you understand? We
must!"

"Listen, Juan. Do you think me a laggard on the
point of honor?"

"Por Dios, no!"

"Then content you; I am as keen on this enterprise as you."

He stared at me for a moment, then broke into
a laugh.

"You conceal your eagerness well," he said.
"However, so be it. But, by the Hand of St. John,
I hope ere I die to see you forget yourself in a mo-
ment of excitement."

Sir Oliver was somewhat reluctant to lend his
precious optic glass, but on my telling him what I
had in mind, and vowing to bring the instrument
back safe, he consented, and Juan and I set out.

The lines of investment were not yet drawn about
St. Angelo and St. Michael, so with a trifle of cir-
cumspection it was easy enough to slip out from Il

76

Borgo and make our way across country toward the southern end of the island. Of course we took care not to expose ourselves on the sky-line, and twice we lay perdu in hollows of the ground while parties of Turkish men-at-arms passed within a few score paces of us, but in the main we had no trouble.

We found good cover on a slope between the casal of Zeitun and St. Thomas' Bay, and there we stretched out while de la Mara took the glass and scanned the camp for Yussef's tent. At length he picked it up and pointed it out to me, with the triple horsetail standard which marked it for that of an aga. With the glass I examined the whole terrain, casting over in my mind various plans of attack, until in the end I settled on one which seemed to hold some promise of success, and outlined it to Juan, who nodded.

"It should work, Ricardo mio," he agreed. "And now to get the Grand Master's permission."

"Which same," I commented, dryly, "may be difficult."

It proved easier than I expected, for la Vallette, after hearing my description of the ground and the outline of my plan, readily gave his consent. I suspect that he owned some secret fondness for me, due either to his having snatched me from the Inquisition or to my prompt obedience in the matter of the poison.

"But no rashness, Sir Richard," he warned me. "If you find that it cannot be done in reasonable safety, I command that you return. How many will you take?"

"Four only," I replied. "If four cannot do it with this plan, neither can four hundred. De la Mara, myself, Hamilcar Xuereb, and David Evans." I had a reason for choosing each of these, as will be seen.

"Very good," said the Grand Master, and thanking him, I withdrew.

I found Juan and told him the result, to his huge delight, and we sent for Xuereb and Evans, to whom, with de la Mara, I assigned each his duties. They also were vastly pleased, Evans grinning broadly, while the Maltese, even as I talked, drew from his girdle his great knife and from his pocket a whetstone, wherewith he fell to sharpening the steel. I appointed a rendezvous, and sent the commoners to their tasks, then tried to persuade de la Mara to take a little rest, since we had another all-night expedition before us. But he professed himself too excited to sleep, so going to my quarters I undressed and lay down, telling my servant to call me at dusk.

The moon, though beginning to wane, still gave ample light for our enterprise, and we were able to make good time, especially since it was not necessary to observe such caution as during the day. By the

78

grace of Heaven, Yussef's tent was near the northern border of the camp and only a few yards from a wied, one of the water-courses which carry the torrential rains of Malta to the sea. It was on these facts, together with the further circumstance of the wied being dry, that my plan was based.

Coming to the wied a mile or so from the Moslem camp, we climbed down into it, and thereafter made our way secure from observation unless chance brought someone to the gully's very rim. However, that was a risk we had to take, and but a slight one, since no Moslem will voluntarily be abroad at night; he knows too well that the dark hours are given over to the demons of the air. And doubtless St. John had us in his keeping, for none saw us.

Reconnoitring from time to time, I led my men along until opposite our goal, then bade them lie down and wait for dawn. The Chevalier de Medrano, who was with Sir Oliver when I returned the optic glass, had advised that hour.

"The foe will then be least alert," he said. "And you, not being sodden with sleep, will be keen and wide awake. Wait till there is light enough to discern what you are about; that is the ideal time for a camisado, a night attack. And God and the saints prosper you! Are you jealous of glory, or will you accept a volunteer?"

"I should be vastly honored to have you," I told

him, heartily. But the Grand Master had other duties for him, so de Medrano was not with us.

Now we settled to our vigil in the shadow of sundry rocks and bushes, Evans offering me some of his eternal Indian weed, which I refused with disgust. He had once persuaded me to try it, proclaiming it a sovereign balm in times of stress, but I was made violently sick by it, and lost all desire to become proficient in the art. Chuckling at my refusal, he crammed it into his own mouth, and proceeded to enjoy himself.

Lying there, we could hear the noises of the camp all about us; the stamp and whicker of horses, the calls of the sentries, the raucous snores of sleeping men, and—or so I thought—the sobbing of a woman in a nearby tent. Presently a rough voice growled something, and the sobbing ended. The moon sank from sight, and we lay in thick darkness, but after a time the stars began to pale, and I knew that dawn was near. Rousing myself, I was conscious of a thin mist creeping up from the sea, and for this I gave thanks; a good fog would mightily aid us in our camisado, and I took this as a sign of God's favor on our attempt. Touching my companions, I warned them to be ready, and realized that I could see clearly enough to make out their forms—the time was at hand.

Now that we were about to put our fortunes to the touch, I felt a tense eagerness, a thrill of excitement, sweep over me, and my heart began thumping madly. Creeping up the side of the wied, with Xuereb beside me, I peered between two bushes that somewhat screened my head. There was the double tent of Yussef, looming vaguely in the mist, and in the rear compartment, the inner room, so to speak, a lamp glowed yellow, casting a wide blotch of light against the cloth. In front, a sentry paced up and down, toward us and away again, almost disappearing in the mist at the farther end of his beat. I watched him through three or four turns, then glanced down to make sure that the Maltese was ready. He was, and nodded, and I saw the heavy knife gleam in his hand. Stretching out my arm, I waited, then as the sentry reached the near end of his beat, not five paces from us, and turned, I motioned quickly. Instantly Xuereb rose to his feet, with the knife poised back of his shoulder, and as he came erect his arm swept forward and the glittering blade flew through the air, turning over and over as it went, to bury itself hilt deep between the sentry's shoulders. Without a cry, the man pitched forward on his face, and Juan, the Maltese, and I, scrambling from the wied, ran to our appointed tasks. According to command, Evans remained where he was, but I waited to make sure that he had drawn flint and steel and was lighting a slow match.

This delayed me long enough to let me see a huge black eunuch rush from the tent, scimitar in hand, and him Juan spitted like a lark. For myself, I split the rearward tent from top to bottom with my dagger, and leaped through the opening. A lamp swung from the peak, and by its light I saw three women start up on their couches, staring at me wide-eyed.

"Est-ce qu'il y a ici une dame française?" I demanded and one of them sprang to her feet, crying:

"C'est moi! Etes-vous des Chevaliers de St. Jehan?"

"Mais oui. A votre secours," * I answered, and at that instant a giant burst into the tent, shouting something that sounded like:

"Ya Allah!" †

I flew at him with my dagger, but he caught my wrist and twisted it so that the weapon dropped from my hand; I was like a child in his grasp. He flung me back, swung up the scimitar he carried— and by the mercy of God it struck the ridgepole of the tent. Before he could recover, I leaped in, drove my foot into his stomach, and as with an explosive grunt he doubled toward me I swung both

---

* "Is there a French lady here?"
"It is I. Are you Knights of St. John?"
"Yes. To your rescue."
† "By God!"

fists with all my force, right and left, on his jaw.
I felt the bone smash under the impact, and as the
giant toppled forward I knew that he was safe; it
would be some time ere he regained consciousness.

"Suivez-moi!" * I cried to the Frenchwoman, and
rushed from the tent, she following close.

Juan and Xuereb were fighting with three or four
Turks, but as I called they abandoned the fight and
leaped with me into the water-course; Evans joined
us, and away the five of us ran, heading for St.
Angelo.

We pressed on as fast as we might, the kindly
mist hiding us from our enemies, but the woman
could not make the speed that we men could, and
we were forced to adjust our gait to hers. She
wore the loose waist and baggy trousers of the
Turkish women, so was not hampered by skirts, but
her light, heelless slippers were never made for stony
ground. She was vigorous, active, and brave, uttering no complaint, but I could see that she was suffering cruelly, and in spite of all the aid that de la
Mara and I could give, our flight was dangerously
slow. We could hear shouts and cries in the camp
behind us, and at length it was clear from the
sounds, gradually drawing nearer, that our pur-
suers had taken to the wied and were gaining on us.
Presently Evans spoke:

* "Follow me!"

"It is time, Sir Richard, for my share of the enterprise."

I nodded, saying:

"Rejoin us later. You can overtake us."

He dropped behind, and we others pressed on. In a few moments, happening to glance back, I saw the mist light up with a yellow glare, and the crash of an explosion smote our ears, followed by shrieks of agony and terror. Another explosion, and another, and the sounds of pursuit died away. Half a mile farther on, Evans caught up with us. He was grinning from ear to ear, and remarked, with evident satisfaction:

"A hand-bomb is a potent discourager. At least I learned something during my stay with the infidel dogs. Would that I could send them all to howl in the fiery ditch of Jehannam!"

Coming to the higher ground, we found the mist dropping away, until by the time the sun was fully up the air was clear and we could see for miles. The blue Mediterranean lay below us, sparkling in the morning light, and involuntarily I halted to glance at the beauty of the scene. But it was no time to admire Nature's loveliness, and we must look for cover. We managed to conceal ourselves, but it was plain that our rescued lady suffered intensely from the bruising her feet had taken on the stones. She made no lamentations, but she limped badly,

84

and her face twisted in pain. On one of our halts
to let her rest, Xuereb spoke to me, and I translated
his words to her.

"He says he has often carried his children pickaback, and you are not much heavier than they. He
wishes to carry you."

She put her head back and laughed, the prettiest
little trill imaginable.

"Il est très gentil, le gros," she said. "How do
you say it in English—you are English, n'est ce pas?
He is very kind—that is it—very kind, this big man.
Eh bien, I accept."

She had evidently ridden pickaback, and not so
many years agone, for as Xuereb handed me his
knife and turned his back she placed her hands on
his shoulders and sprang, clipping him about the
waist with her thighs. He hooked his forearms
under her knees, clasped his fingers, and she clasped
her hands across his broad chest. She laughed
again, and chirped in his ear, as one does to a horse.

"He makes a fine charger," she said to me. "I
could well wish to ride into battle on such a one."

I translated this to the Maltese, who grinned de-
lightedly and nodded, and so, Juan and I scouting
ahead and Evans bringing up the rear, we made our
way toward Il Borgo.

By and by the lady called me back to her side and

spoke to me, using the English well, with just the faintest trace of accent.

"I am the Lady Madeleine d'Armagnac, of France," she said. "May I know your names?"

"I am Sir Richard Ayresford, of England, at your service," I told her. "This, the Chevalier Juan de la Mara, of Aragon. This, David Evans, likewise of England; and he on whom you ride is Hamilcar Xuereb, of Malta."

She acknowledged the introductions, then asked: "How chanced you four in the Turkish camp?"

"We came for you," I replied, but she begged: "Nay, Sir Richard, prithee do not jest with me."

"It is the simple truth. We learned that a Christian lady was held by the infidel, and we enterprised her rescue."

"You four alone?"

"We four alone."

She stared at me for a moment, then blinked rapidly, and two tears rolled down her cheeks, while her lips quivered.

"You are in truth very brave and gallant chevaliers," she said. "I had resigned myself to a dreadful fate . . . perchance I may at some time thank you properly . . . not now. . . ." And she turned away, resting her forehead on Xuereb's mighty shoulder.

Coming to Il Borgo, the lady insisted on dismounting, feeling that it did not comport with her dignity to be carried like a child through the streets of the town, for the mirth of the common folk. So she walked with us to St. Angelo, where, shortly after matins, we ushered her into the presence of the Grand Master.

Then, to our astonishment and dismay, she collapsed, weeping as though her heart would break—she, who had hitherto been so brave and so enduring!—until la Vallette sent a messenger post-haste for a noblewoman of the town, one Countess Carmela de Zerafa, who, coming to our aid, assured us that the lady was merely over-wrought, and would recover with rest. Full of tenderness and pity, the countess led her away to the Zerafa Palace in Il Borgo, and Juan and I were called upon to relate our adventure to the Grand Master and such of the Order as chanced to be present. The Knights pressed about us with heartiest congratulations and generous approval, and la Vallette sent for Evans and Xuereb to receive his personal commendation. This done, he dismissed us, saying:

"There will, doubt it not, be other opportunities to show your mettle, so get you some repose while still you may; the time is at hand when there will be but little rest for any within these walls."

CHAPTER IV

Of the Siege of St. Elmo; and How the Dog Pierrot Saved My Life

THE Countess de Zerafa spoke truly, for it was not more than a day or two ere Juan and I were summoned to receive the thanks of the Lady Madeleine, who was staying at the Zerafa Palace. The two women had struck up a great friendship, being in truth not unlike in both appearance and character, and when we were introduced into one of the smaller rooms of the palace we found them both awaiting us.

The Lady Madeleine was vastly changed from the somewhat dishevelled, foot-sore, and anxious person whom we had brought back from the Turkish camp. Rest had done wonders for her, and now, her dark hair neatly arranged and gathered in a silver net, her Turkish garb replaced by a robe of the countess', she received us with all the dignity of her lofty blood. She was perhaps a year or two younger than myself, and was indeed a lovely woman, beautiful with the dark, fiery beauty of the South, and in the main grave and reserved, though her brown eyes filled with tears as she gave thanks to Juan and me.

It does not become me to repeat her words; suffice it to say that she over-praised us until for very shame we protested that we had done no more than our simple duty.

"How can you say that?" was her reply. "In truth, it was a most courageous and knightly rescue, not to be underrated by the doers thereof. I can see plainly that you are very gallant chevaliers. Is it not so, Carmela?"

The countess agreed, adding:

"But after all, it is no more than one would expect of the Knights of St. John. When you know them better you will learn that it is against their tradition to count danger." She gave us each a hand, and as we bent to kiss them she went on: "You must come to see us often, gentlemen, when your duties permit. Madeleine will stay with me during the siege, being alone in the world, even as I am." The countess was a childless widow, in the middle twenties; she was married young, her husband being a good friend of the Order, though of course not a member. He fell in the siege of Mazarquivir, two years before this time, since when the countess had lived alone—save for her servants—in the Zerafa Palace. "Her father and brother were slain," the countess pursued, "by the Turkish

89

raiders who took her captive. When this war is over, she can return to her home in France; meanwhile she is my guest. . . . Oh, yes! one other thing. May I ask that you will divide this between the two brave men who aided you?"

She handed me a purse of gold coins, and though we protested that neither Evans nor Xuereb had acted in hope of a reward, she insisted.

"It will not come amiss," she laughed. "They can get nobly drunk on this, which, I gather, is the chief delight of the soldier."

We laughed also, admitting that she was not far wrong, and after a further exchange of compliments, Juan and I withdrew.

On the way back to our posts, Juan congratulated me.

"You have made a conquest, Ricardo mio," he said. "And such a conquest! Sangre de Cristo! Is she not beautiful, the Lady Madeleine? So graceful, so dignified, so high-bred—and so exquisite! Oriana, beloved of Amadis of Gaul, was never half so fair. And she adores you—Ricardo, my felicitations! It is you big, tawny Englishmen who have the ladies at your feet."

"Be not so foolish, Juan," I told him. "She has seen me but twice."

"And she worships the ground on which you tread—in sooth, the little god's arrows fly swiftly! Did you not see the way she looked at you? Alas, that I had your way with the fair! Ay de mi!"

"Besides," I rejoined, "my heart and my honor are engaged in England."

"Your honor, perchance. But can your heart remain indifferent to the most exquisite Lady Madeleine? And when she so plainly is yours for the grasping?"

"Your Aragonese imagination runs riot, my friend. And you do the lady but little honor—"

"Nay, I meant no discourtesy to her; of course she loves you honorably! Aught else is unthinkable."

"Still," I admitted, "there is no denying that she is beautiful and charming."

He snorted contemptuously.

"Take care not to over-praise her, in your mad enthusiasm! However, that is no small concession, from one with the blood of a fish in his veins."

And there the argument ended.

As the Grand Master had predicted, the Turks made no attempt, at first, to invest St. Angelo or St. Michael, but concentrated their efforts on St. Elmo. They planted a battery on the point north of the castle, and this did some damage, but their main attack was on the landward side. The rocky nature of the ground kept them from digging trenches, but all across the promontory, between St.

Elmo and Mount Sceberras, they erected a double breastwork of planks and logs, filling the space between with earth. Behind this breastwork they sheltered their smaller guns, placing the larger ones farther back toward the hill, and I learned that Cassar had not exaggerated the size of the Moslem artillery. Rather, he had understated it, for one of their huge basilicas cast stone bullets a cubit in diameter, weighing twice as much as a man.

St. Elmo mounted thirty guns, most of them now brought over to the landward side, but though the defenders worked these manfully, the Turks had more than double the number, and the walls of the fortress began to crumble under the terrific rain of stone and iron which was hurled upon them. The bombardment opened. on the twenty-fourth of May, six days after the invaders landed, and by the first of June it was clear that the fort must in the end be taken. The Knights within the castle accordingly met, discussed the matter, and deputed the Chevalier de la Cerda to cross over to St. Angelo and beg assistance of the Grand Master.

A subterranean gallery ran from a point within St. Elmo to a spot near the shore of the Grand Harbor, its mouth being well concealed among rocks and bushes on the western slope of Mount Sceberras. Through this passage, which was unknown to the Turks, la Cerda made his way, presenting himself before la Vallette and asking aid. The Grand Master summoned a Council of the Grand Crosses, and I attended, for though only Knights of Justice might vote at these councils, Associates were as a rule allowed to be present; only when some secret matter was to be discussed were we excluded.

When all were assembled, la Cerda was invited to speak, and with some hesitation he did so.

"Grand Master and Knights of the Order," he began, "I am come to ask succor for St. Elmo. For a week, now, our defences have been crumbling, bit by bit, under the Moslem guns; indeed, had they not been hewn, in great part, from the living rock, they could not have held out so long. We must have aid if we are to make good the place."

It was clear that this request, coming so early in the siege, was displeasing to la Vallette; his face showed as much, as did also the coldness of his voice when he inquired:

"How many of the defenders have fallen?"

La Cerda did not reply directly.

"St. Elmo," he answered, "is like unto a sick man, who needs the assistance of a chirurgeon."

"I will be your chirurgeon," la Vallette assured him, his manner indifferent, though bordering on harshness. "And I will bring you such help that if I cannot allay your fears I may at least hope to save the place from falling into the hands of the

93

enemy. It is necessary that St. Elmo hold out to the last; the Viceroy of Sicily has promised us aid, but we must gain time for the mustering of his forces. I doubt not that I can find among our Order a sufficiency of gallant men to go with me and bury ourselves in the ruins."

La Cerda flushed hotly, but looked down at the floor and made no response, while a chorus of protest arose from the others. It was not fitting, they said, for the commander to sacrifice himself like a common soldier; he was our leader, to direct the war, not to fight hand-to-hand in the mêlée; who among us could take over the command if he were lost? And so on, over and over.

While all this was taking place, Don Diego stood shoulder to shoulder with me in the press, and now he leaned toward me and spoke in my ear.

"Sir Richard," he said, "if I may presume to mention a thought which has doubtless already occurred to you, here is an opportunity for you to gain the distinction that we both crave. Should you volunteer to return with la Cerda, there is much glory to be won ere St. Elmo falls."

I almost laughed in his face, so transparent was his motive. It is unquestionably true that there was glory to be won, but there was also an excellent prospect that I would lose my life when the castle should finally be taken—and his path to the Lady

Alice would then be cleared. I chuckled inwardly, and said:

"A most excellent plan! Doubtless you also mean to volunteer; we will go together."

"Alas, no!" he replied. "Would that I could do so. But I am with the guns of la Sangle, and my duties forbid me to offer myself."

This time I laughed outright, and stepping forward, I bowed before la Vallette, craving permission to return in company with la Cerda. The Grand Master smiled, saying:

"I commend your spirit, Sir Richard. But be not too forward; it is for the older Knights to offer first."

"Nay," spoke up the Chevalier de Medrano, "I too would be glad to go, and ask no better than to have Sir Richard accompany us. He has shown himself to be a youth of enterprise and stout heart."

It was plain by Espinosa's face that this was gall and wormword to him, but after all he had brought it on himself, and I was not displeased.

A number of other Knights spoke up, clamoring to go, and in the end it was decided that fifty of the Order, with two companies of Maltese soldiers, should be placed under command of Medrano, for the aid of the besieged. That very night we were set across the harbor in open boats, with stores of food and ammunition, while a heavy fire from the guns of St. Angelo protected us as we landed. Reaching the shore, we made our way to the mouth of the underground passage, and in no long time were within the walls of St. Elmo.

During our passage, something occurred to the advantage of the Order. The Turkish admiral, Pialé, was endeavoring to rally his men for an attack on our party when a shot from St. Angelo, striking a stone, broke off a splinter which wounded him severely. We saw him fall, and raised a cheer, while the Turks, thrown into confusion by the loss of their leader, gave over all thought of interfering with us. Unfortunately, Pialé was not killed, but it was a fortnight or more ere he was able to take part in the siege. And la Vallette profited by the confusion following this incident to despatch a swift galley to Sicily, begging the viceroy to hasten the succours he had promised us. To this Don Garcia de Toledo replied that aid would reach us not later than the middle of June; how the faint-hearted traitor kept his word shall be told later.

The Chevalier de Medrano was at this time about thirty-five or thirty-six years of age—old enough to be sagacious in warfare, but young enough to have still the fire and dash of youth. This fact he proved on the morning after our entry into the fort, when, calling the Knights together, he demanded that we make a sally against the besiegers. The aged de

Broglio objected, and some of the less courageous defenders felt, with him, that it would be a useless waste of life, but de Medrano overbore them.

"The best defence is ever a sudden and unexpected attack," he told us. "If we can inflict some damage on the infidels, convince them that we do not fear them, and perhaps spike some of their guns, we shall have done more good than by skulking within the fort." Some of the Knights frowned at the word "skulking," but de Medrano gave them no opportunity to object, and continued: "The stoutest defence of the holy St. John is not in these walls of stone, but in the hearts and arms of his warriors."

We younger Knights supported this view, and that very afternoon a band of us made ready for the outfall. There were some forty Knights and five or six hundred Maltese volunteers in the party, and we made a brave show as we gathered in the outer fosse, the men of the Order in cuirass and glittering headpiece, their scarlet surcoats bearing the white cross of St. John, and the commoners in leathern jerkin and cap, with here and there a morion or burgonet, acquired God only knew how. Of the common soldiers, perhaps a hundred were arquebusiers, blowing on the matches of their cumbrous weapons, the rest being armed with pike and knife; we of the Order, of course, used sword and dagger, though some few carried in addition a pair of the

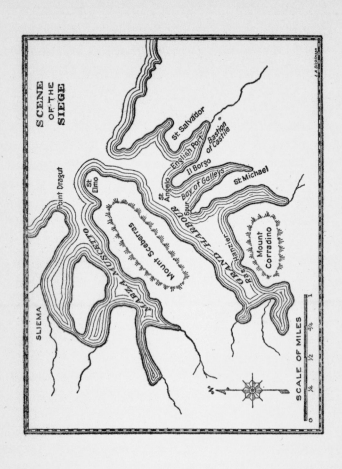

SCENE OF THE SIEGE

SLIEMA

Point Dragut

St. Elmo

MARZA MUSCETTO

Mount Sceberras

St. Salvador

English Point

Bastion of Castille

Il Borgo

St. Angelo

Bay of Galleys

St. Michael

GRAND HARBOUR

Spur of Bourg

Fort Ricasoli

Mount Corradino

SCALE OF MILES

0   ¼   ½   ¾   1

new wheel-lock hand-guns thrust into their belts.

When all was ready, de Medrano ordered the trumpets to sound, and we climbed from the fosse and set out at a moderate run for the infidel lines. All night long, and through the morning hours, the bombardment had gone on unabated, the explosions of the musketry blending into one long-drawn roar, punctuated by the deep boom of cannon. Solid shot and bombs pounded against the walls or burst with tearing noise inside the ramparts, and for many weary weeks we were to know this deafening thunder, with now and then a crash of falling masonry, as a background to our daily lives, though later in the siege it changed its character; when more of the heavy guns came into play the note grew deeper, heavier, with the musketry seeming, by comparison, to snap and crackle. The smoke of the guns lay foul and sulphurous in pools along the ground, or, borne by the moving air, drifted slowly down toward the sea. This too was to become familiar to us as time went on.

The nearest of the besiegers' positions lay scarce two hundred paces from our fosse, and we covered the distance before the Paynim dogs knew well what was on foot. Their musketry did some harm, it is true, but we swarmed over their breastworks and were among them ere they could gather to repel us. This was my first experience of a mêlée, and I carry

but detached recollections of it—de Medrano crying: "For God and St. John!" as he ran a Turk
through the body; a swarthy infidel heaving up
his scimitar for a blow at me, and the look of astonishment on his face when my sword passed through
him; another aiming a musket at the head of a
Knight, and himself falling when the gun burst in
his face. And over all the roar of gunfire, the
stench of sulphur, and the shouts of the fighters—
"St. John! St. John!" "St. Iago y cierra, España!" *
"Ya Allah! Allaho akbar!" †

It was a short battle, but savage while it lasted,
and we drove the Moslems from a considerable portion of their works. We dismounted a number of
their guns, and spiked others, but these were the
smaller ones, falconets and sakers; the huge basilicas, farther up the slope, were beyond our reach.
While we were thus engaged, the besiegers rallied,
attacked us in front and on both flanks, and in turn
drove us back to St. Elmo. However, we were well
satisfied; we had done some damage, had slain a
goodly number of the Paynim hounds, and had ourselves suffered but little; more, we had planted in
their minds the knowledge that we could strike back.

Again within our ramparts, we were enjoying a
breathing-space when a fresh alarm called us once
more to the fight. A Turkish officer, reconnoitring

* "St. James and charge, Spain!"
† "Oh, God! God is greatest!"

our defences, noted that the sentinel had left a certain portion of the counterscarp, and under cover of the drifting smoke, borne down upon us by a faint breeze, the Turks delivered an attack on that point. Ere we fully knew what was on hand, they had made good their footing, and the banner of the Crescent floated over that part of our works. The infidels were collecting there to launch an attack on our ravelin, but de Medrano and the Bailiff of Negropont gathered us together and delivered a counterattack which stopped them short. But try as we might, we could not drive the invaders from their position, and their accursed banner still floated from our outer wall. Again and again we swept in to the assault, and as often they flung us off, till in the fifth attack I took a scimitar on my head and knew nothing more until I opened my eyes in the hospital in Il Borgo.

The main ward, where I lay, was a long, dark room, hung with purple velvet curtains, and with but few windows, and those small; it is well known that excessive light is bad for the sick, and the hospital was built with that in mind. I lay in a great four-post bed, with a dark canopy above, and my first thought was that I was in the lower world of which Vergilius Maro tells us, for through the gloom I could hear on every hand half-stifled moans of pain, and smothered curses, with a grumbling under-note which puzzled me until I knew it for the roar of the guns at St. Elmo. Then slowly my wits came back, and I recognized the place for what it was. My head ached and was sore, and I stirred restlessly. At once a face appeared at my bedside, and a voice inquired:

"What is it, Sir Richard? Is there something you wish? The saints be praised, you have come back to us!"

It was the Countess Carmela, and she laid a cool and infinitely soothing hand on my forehead.

"Is there water?" I asked, and with one hand she lifted my head, while with the other she held a goblet to my lips. Some acid juice had been mixed with the drink, making it vastly refreshing, so that after a deep draught I felt much better.

"How came I here?" I asked.

She lowered my head to the pillow.

"You must not talk," she admonished me. "You were wounded in the fighting, and Xuereb and another carried you through the underground way, bringing you here, along with sundry others. Now try to sleep."

"One question. Does St. Elmo still stand?"

"It does, and by God's grace will stand for many a day."

I gave thanks to God, then said:

"I think I could sleep if . . ."

"If what?"

"If you would sit by me and hold my hand . . . my head aches . . . am I too bold?"

She laughed gently.

"A sick man is naught more than an overgrown child. There, mother's baby shall have his hand held!"

My right hand lay in hers, while with the fingers of her left she stroked my temples, and in no time I found myself drifting off on pleasant clouds of sleep.

Waking, I found that the countess had deserted me, her place being taken by the Lady Madeleine, who from then on seemed to have elected herself my special nurse.

"We women have taken over the care of the wounded," she told me. "Yes, I know it is the allotted task of the Knights, but every sword is needed for battle—and would you have us sit idle, with folded hands?"

"I am more than glad that you have done so," I assured her. "I would far rather be cared for by you than by some heavy-fisted warrior. Apart from which, you are vastly pleasanter to look upon."

She wrinkled her nose at me.

"Fie, Sir Richard!" she chided. "Is it the part of a true knight to flatter a lonely damsel, to overwhelm her with honeyed words? And you betrothed in England! Fie, for shame!"

But she was only teasing, and I laughed with her.

I had lain for twenty hours unconscious, she told me, until my life was despaired of. But this evening the chirurgeon went his rounds, and stopping by my bed declared me out of danger, provided due care was used in my recovery. He was a pleasant, round-faced man of Italy, Messer Girolamo Gaddi by name, not one of the Knights, but a Serving Brother of the Order.

"Ha!" he said. "Our traveler returns. You have cheated the devil for the nonce, Sir Richard." He felt my pulse and forehead. "Si, si! You will live to do much harm yet."

"No good?" I asked, plaintively, and he shook his head, chuckling.

"It were too much to hope! But you are in good hands. Keep him quiet, Lady Madeleine. And mind, Sir Richard, no leaping from bed and calling for your arms until I give the word."

He was a worthy follower of Hippocrates, there is no question, and he wrought many marvellous cures among the sick and wounded. But he had some strange ideas, at variance with the best practice. For one thing, he refused flatly to bleed a man fevered from wounds.

"Is it logic?" he would say. "Tell me, is it logic? For sickness, perhaps, but for wounds, no. Consider! A man has lost blood, therefore he is fevered. And to reduce his fever, we are to take still more blood from him. Pah! Were this true, a Moslem scimitar were the ideal cure for wounds. Beyond which, observation teaches the folly of such a course. And I am none so sure that it is best for disease; I remain unconvinced."

"But do not the wisest physicians prescribe it?" I asked him once.

"The wisest physicians are fools!" he snorted. "Owls! Bats! Idiots! Because it has always been done, therefore it must always be done—quod erat demonstrandum! The saints deliver me from such logic!"

Another of his odd notions was that a sick or wounded man should be bathed all over daily with tepid water, and he insisted on this for each and every patient. Although the Lady Madeleine was my regular nurse, this task she delegated to the Countess Carmela, and I may say that I blushed from head to foot the first time that it was done— nor, if the crimson that flooded her cheeks may be taken for a sign, was the countess wholly free from embarrassment. But I must admit that the bath was both soothing and refreshing, so that I came to look forward to it.

The day after I regained my senses, a visitor was announced, and whom should it prove to be but de la Mara. He had been asking for me a dozen times at least, Lady Madeleine told me, and was well-nigh beside himself with joy when finally admitted. He was allowed to stay only a few minutes, but the clasp of his hand and the look on his face told more than volumes of speech could have done.

"You must make haste and get strong, Ricardo mio," he said. "Still, he that gives must take, and by what Medrano says you have more than squared your account. And who could blame you for prolonging your illness, with such a nurse? But there is much glory still to be won; St. Elmo holds out, but it grows weaker day by day.

"Out with you!" broke in Lady Madeleine. "I will not have you exciting my patient with your talk of war. Out! And come not back until you can speak soothing instead of stirring words."

Relentlessly she drove him from the room, while I lay and smiled at the look of dismay on his countenance.

David Evans came to see me also, twisting his cap in his hands with the embarrassment of trying to find something to say, and with the further distress of wondering where to spit; he had forgotten to rid his mouth of the Indian herb ere entering. At length, in desperation, and as I thought him about to drown, he gulped a huge swallow of the juice, and spoke.

"I am right glad, Sir Richard, to see you in such good health . . . I . . . I . . ." And with that he turned and rushed from the room, Lady Madeleine sending her laughter on his heels.

The Grand Master, on his daily rounds of the hospital, stopped for a word with me, and Don Diego de Espinosa came to call, expressing regret over my wound.

"I reproach myself, Sir Richard," he said, "for that it was at my suggestion that you volunteered for St. Elmo. Had I not spoken, this wound of yours might still be in the limbo of things unknown. I trust that you will forgive me?"

"There is naught to forgive," I assured him. "We are in the midst of war, and one cannot make an omelet without breaking eggs." I was beginning to catch Juan's trick of speaking in proverbs. "If not then, some other time."

"You are very good," he murmured. "I fear that in like case I might not prove so generous."

Oddest of all my visitors was Hamilcar Xuereb— odd, I should say, for his errand, not for himself. Late one afternoon, I woke from a nap, to see standing beside my bed a huge man who carried a naked scimitar. For a moment, in the half light, I fancied that some Turk had made his way into the hospital to slay me, and my heart thumped madly while I planned to hurl my pillow at him and roll out from the other side of the bed. Then I saw who it was, and greeted him pleasantly, being inwardly amused at my own folly.

"Good day, Hamilcar," I said, to which he responded, eagerly:

"Good day, Sir Richard. It is a joy to see you so far recovered. And I bring you a gift to aid you back to health." He lifted the scimitar in both hands, offering it to me. "I was nearby when you were struck down, and though not near enough to ward the blow, I finished the dog of an infidel who gave it, and have brought you his weapon." And he laid it on the bed beside me.

I thanked him for the gift, adding:

"It will make an interesting souvenir."

Messer Gaddi approaching just then, I told him of Xuereb's present, but the Maltese had something further to say.

"Nay, Sir Richard, it is more than a remembrance." He searched his garments, producing a box of some aromatic substance. "If you will but anoint the blade, and especially the edge, with this ointment, made for me by a wise woman of Gozo, it will vastly speed the healing of your wound. Is it not so?" he appealed to the physician.

Messer Gaddi snorted.

"Sympathetic magic!" he replied. "Akin to that other common superstition of the vulgar, which makes a wax doll of an enemy and sticks pins into it, to compass the death of the living person. One might as well anoint the stones of St. Angelo for Sir Richard's welfare."

"Nay, but I myself have seen that done," expostulated Xuereb. "The crippling of a man by thrusting pins into his image. It is a fact; I have seen it happen, good sir."

"Post hoc, ergo propter hoc—after this, therefore because of this," snorted the chirurgeon. "We stick pins into the image of a man; the man dies; therefore it was the pins that slew him. And God and St. John might talk till Doomsday to convince you of your error!"

"Then you will not use my ointment?" Xuereb was so clearly chagrined that I took pity on him.

"Nay, good Hamilcar," I said, "of a certainty I will use it. And my thanks for your kindness." At this he beamed delight. "A word in your ear," I went on. "These men of science are wise, in good sooth, but they do not know all that is to be known. I also have seen marvels wrought."

After some further chat, Xuereb withdrew, vastly pleased with himself and with me; the surest way to keep a man's allegiance is to let him do something for you. Messer Gaddi bent a sardonic eye upon me.

"And you to fall victim to a belief in magic arts!" he mourned, half jokingly. "I had given you credit for intelligence above the average, Sir Richard. What comes to us is from God and the blessed saints, not from wise women and sorcerers, with their loathesome concoctions of bats' tongues, toads' eyes, and the like."

"Nay," I laughed, "I trust it as little as you do.

But Xuereb is a good man, and if by humoring him I can keep his loyalty, I am willing to pretend somewhat. And at least it can do no harm to have the signs on our side, in our favor."

"Humph!" he grunted. "It is beneath the dignity of a man of science to notice such fairy-tales. However, so be it; I will aid you to humor him. Give hither the witch's salve, and I will anoint the blade—to the greater glory of God and the swift healing of your wound," he added, sardonically.

Thus by a trifle of duplicity—pardonable, I trust —I kept the loyalty of two good men.

But my most constant and attentive companion was the Lady Madeleine. She sat beside me, brought me food and cooling drinks, changed the dressings on my wound, turned my pillow to present a cool surface to my head, fanned the flies away from me, and talked of her girlhood or listened while I talked. Thus I told her of my youth in England, of the death of my parents—whereat her lips quivered and she gripped my hand—and of the Lady Alice and how she had sent me off to war, though I thought to observe a certain lack of sympathy here. And I learned of Lady Madeleine's home, of the death of her mother, and the full tale of the slaying of her father and brother in the raid wherein she was taken.

"We should be friends," she told me, "inasmuch

as we are both alone in the world. Save that mere
friendship seems weak when one has the cause for
gratitude that is mine."

"Not more than mine," I demurred. "If I
snatched you from slavery, you have drawn me
back from the grave."

But this she denied, holding that my salvation was
wrought by Xuereb and Messer Gaddi, whereupon
we went into an amicable and friendly discussion
as to which owed most to the other.

Also, for hours at a time Lady Madeleine would
read to me of the adventures of Amadis of Gaul,
or from the Orlando Furioso, or perchance of the
Four Sons of Aymon, or Sir Thomas Malorie's
goodly annals of King Arthur. She adored these
tales of chivalry, and though I found them somewhat high-flown and old in fashion, for my part
I loved the tones of her rich contralto voice, and
the sight of her dark, sleek head, with its profile
like some fine-cut cameo, as she bent over the volumes. And I noted a thing which seemed to me
strange; that as time passed, Lady Madeleine's image
seemed to supplant in my mind that of Lady Alice.
It was not that I loved Lady Madeleine, or that
my love for Lady Alice had grown less, but when,
closing my eyes, I tried to vision the English girl,
it was the picture of the French damsel that rose
to view. A curious freak of mind, no doubt, but it

disturbed me, until in the end I gave up thinking about it and put it wholly from me.

I was in the hospital one day short of a fortnight, my wound healing rapidly under the influence of a marvellous balsam of which Messer Gaddi had the secret. He compounded it himself, and it stung horribly when applied (this, I take it, was due to the turpentine which was one of its chief ingredients) but wounds mended quickly from its use, and without the loathesome festering that so often ensues in these cases. Indeed, so far as the wound itself went, I might have returned to service earlier, but I was weak from the loss of blood and from the blow on my skull, wherefore the chirurgeon insisted that I rest for a time and recover strength through good food and rich wine of Portugal, with which the hospital was amply stored. And it was through this matter of food that a most alarming event took place.

Coming to me one morning, the Lady Madeleine showed signs of tears, and I asked the cause.

"It is my Pierrot," she answered. "One day soon after my arrival here, a small dog of the streets adopted me, following me back to the Zerafa Palace. He was so fascinating in his ways that I took him in, named him Pierrot, and in these few days have learned to love him. And now the Grand Master has given orders that all dogs must be slain, since they eat food which may be needed for the garrison." And the tears overflowed her eyes and rolled down her cheeks.

I comforted her as best I might, but there was little I could do save promise that the animal should be put out of the way as mercifully as possible. By now I was spending most of my time in a chair, or walking about the wards, and Lady Madeleine left me while she went to summon Pierrot, that I might make his acquaintance. He came in, a small dog of no distinguishable breed, frisking about and wagging his ridiculous stump of a tail in so friendly a manner that I could easily see how he had captivated her.

"I know he is base-born," said Lady Madeleine. "Of villein birth, I admit. But is he not fascinating? Charming? T'es tout à fait gentil, mon petit! Do but look at his big brown eyes, his absurd snout, his white teeth, and the way in which one ear cocks up and the other down as he turns his head on one side to look at us! And I must lose him!" Again her eyes filled with tears.

We kept Pierrot by us, amusing ourselves with his antics, until Lady Madeleine brought me my nonemeat from the kitchen. Then as she placed the food before me, I said:

"Since Pierrot's fate is sealed, let us at least send him on his way happy. We will give him a goodly meal, and let him depart with his stomach full and with a pleasant memory."

Taking a tranchoir of bread, I placed thereon several pieces of beef, cut to fit the little creature's mouth, together with some vegetables, and set the whole on the floor beside my chair. Pierrot fell to with a will, gulping down the food and following it with the gravy-soaked bread, his tail going madly the while. Lady Madeleine and I watched, smiling at the eagerness with which he relished his victuals, and when he had finished I asked:

"Was it indeed good, Pierrot?" To which he replied with a frisk and a bark.

My own dinner had stood disregarded while we watched the dog, and well for me that it did so, for even as we looked, his tail stopped wagging, he opened his mouth and gasped twice, shuddered, and fell dead.

Lady Madeleine and I stared at each other in amazement, and my first thought was that a bone had caught in his throat, choking him. She flung herself on her knees, lifting the small body in her arms and uttering piteous cries. Then she turned to me aghast, her eyes wide.

"Look!" she said. "Mark the froth on his lips. Poison!" A sudden thought struck her. "Sainte Vierge!" she cried. "Richard, it was meant for you!"

Recalling what we had done to the spring of
Sliema, I thought at once that through some traitor
the Turks had reached our food with intent to
poison all in the hospital—perchance the whole
garrison.

"Run!" I told her. "Stop the others from eating
—summon Messer Gaddi. Speed, speed!"

Hurrying away, she spread the news and brought
the chirurgeon, who examined the dinners of all the
men and ordered them thrown out. The dogs of
Il Borgo held high revel, and Messer Gaddi set men
to watch them, to see if others died. Also, he sent
posthaste for la Vallette, who came and questioned
the hospital cooks, repressing with stern commands
the bustle and excitement which ran like fire through
the whole building. But though the men were separated, the knots of gesticulating talkers broken up,
no orders could stop the under-cover agitation that
prevailed, or end the whispering between man and
man.

One and all the kitchen servants denied all knowledge of anything untoward in the food, whereupon
the Grand Master ordered them all to the question,
but on the way to the torture-chamber one of the
scullions, a man named Casolani, was taken with the
same symptoms Pierrot had shown.

He did not pass so easily as the dog had done;
instead, he writhed about the floor in paroxysms,

calling for a priest to shrive him. La Vallette bent over him, demanding sternly that he confess.

"It was I," groaned the wretched man. "I put the poison in Sir Richard's food—oh, oh, I burn, I die! Absolve me and let me go!"

"You have taken the poison yourself?" asked the Grand Master, and the man replied:

"I dared not face the torture—oh, Father, grant me absolution!"

"Was all the food poisoned?"

"No, only the one dish. As God sees me, only—" Here a fresh spasm griped him and he rolled about, groaning and clutching at his stomach.

"Had you accomplices in your villainy?"

The man shook his head.

"No," he gasped, "I was alone. That is, I was hired—oh, God, have mercy."

It was plain that he was suffering the most frightful agony, and those gathered about looked with horror on his torment.

"Who paid you?" la Vallette insisted. "Confess, if you hope to escape the flames of Hell!"

"Oh God, have pity! They can be no worse than this! I—I—Oh Jesu, pardon me! Receive my soul—oh, Father in Heaven!"

"Absolvo te!" said la Vallette, making the sign of the cross over the man, whose lips drew back in a ghastly grin as he stiffened and died.

The Grand Master stood erect and looked sternly about the ring of faces, some angry, some pitiful, some terrified. But none wore a guilty aspect, and he sent the kitchen servants about their work, the guards to their duties, then with Sir Oliver, Messer Gaddi, and myself, walked back to where Lady Madeleine awaited us. Messer Gaddi's assistants came to report that none of the street dogs had shown distress, and la Vallette nodded.

"With that," he said, "and with Casolani's confession, incomplete though it was, I think we may rest assured that the danger is not general. It is plain, though, Sir Richard, that you have some private enemy; one who bears you a grudge and would be glad of your death."

"But who?" I asked. "I am at feud with none."

The Grand Master shrugged.

"Who can say? You have perchance been harsh with those under you, and one of them, in his twisted brain, has conceived a hatred for you." I shook my head in doubt. "Or," he went on, "it may be that some one would remove you from his path."

At this, of course, I thought of Don Diego, but recognized at once the folly of such an idea—a grandee of Castile to resort to assassination, and by such foul, unknightly means! No, I disliked the man, but I must perforce exonerate him of so base a charge.

"Be certain," la Vallette continued, "that this will be most thoroughly investigated. We cannot allow a traitor to pass undiscovered.

Let me say here that Evans—who had a natural gift for espionage—and three others were set to learn, if they could, who had employed Casolani to scatter the poison. But naught came of it; the villain remained hidden, and I was convinced that actually there was none such—that he was in sooth a figment of delirium in the suffering man's disordered brain. But to return.

"Give thanks to God, Sir Richard," said la Vallette, "that He has so marvellously protected you. How chanced it that you did not eat the food?" I told him, and he smiled. "Your kindly act met a swift reward," he said. "Poor Pierrot! But since his fate was decreed, he has served a good turn in saving you. I am not of those who hold that the lower creatures cannot, with merit, be admitted into the Kingdom of Heaven—I have known dogs that deserved such recompense more than some men— and doubtless the good St. John has by now taken Pierrot under his special care. At least we may hope and believe so." And he smiled kindly at Lady Madeleine, who smiled back at him through her tears.

"Do you still desire service in St. Elmo?" continued la Vallette, to me.

"Indeed, yes! And I am fully recovered, sir."

The Grand Master looked inquiringly at Messer Gaddi, who nodded.

"Very well, Sir Richard. You may return to duty there to-morrow. And your fellows will be glad of your aid, being sore pressed. While you have been in hospital, the famous Dragut, Pasha of Tripoli, whom the infidels know by the name of Torgud, has brought thirteen galleys and some ten thousand men to the siege, and has planted four more culverins on the eastern point of Marza Muscetto. Some of the wounded men will return to-night, and to-morrow I am sending others to replace them, under the Chevalier de Miranda. You can go with the reinforcements." This was indeed an honor, for de Miranda was one of the most brilliant and illustrious members of the Order, a soldier not only of unlimited personal courage, but of military skill second to none, and a man of great charm, so that I thrilled at being included in his party. "To-morrow at dusk," the Grand Master concluded.

And with Sir Oliver and Messer Gaddi accompanying him, he departed, while Lady Madeleine went in search of a dinner to replace the one which had so nearly cost me my life.

CHAPTER V

Of the Mutiny of St. Elmo; and the Fight in the Catacombs

IT was not, however, my fate to go with the Chevalier de Miranda, for even while his expedition was making ready, an event occurred which delayed my return to St. Elmo. But before I tell of that, I must give some account of how matters stood with the fortress, and of the regrettable conduct of certain among the defenders, together with the manner in which la Vallette brought them back to their duty.

The redoubtable corsair who brought aid to the besiegers was famed throughout Islam—and, indeed, through no small part of Christendom as well—as an engineer no less than as a naval commander, so that Pialé and Mustapha listened with utmost respect to his advice. He at once insisted that St. Elmo must be cut off from all communication with St. Angelo, and as the first step toward this he established a battery of heavy guns on a headland north of the latter fortress, this battery dividing its attentions between the two castles. His own personal camp was also placed here, and the headland, taking its name from him, has since been known as Point Dragut.

Bombardment followed by assaults placed both counterscarp and ravelin of St. Elmo in the hands of the Turks, forcing the defenders to retire within the castle itself, and enabling the infidels to batter the naked walls of the fortress at short range. So savage and unremitting, indeed, was the artillery practice that the Knights were obliged to construct intrenchments within the walls, for shelter from the rain of stone and iron which was poured on them. Day and night, with no remission, that terrible gun-fire went on, shaking the very foundations of the island with its thunder, nor could any masonry hope long to withstand so frightful a tempest; little by little the walls were eaten away. The defenders labored stoutly to repair the damage, but many of them were slain, more were wounded, and one and all were worn down by toil and exhausted from their protracted watching, from the long-drawn strain of anxiety.

In this dreadful position, it is perhaps not strange that for a time their courage faltered—nay, let me not do them an injustice even in thought. Let me say, rather, that they felt they had done all their duty required; that they might honorably withdraw from a post which could not be held. Nor was it all of the Knights who felt thus; de Broglio, the

Bailiff of Negropont, and many of the older Brethren were staunchly obedient to the Grand Master's orders, but some of the younger ones felt that they were being sacrificed to no good purpose. Having this in mind, they sent the Chevalier de Medrano to la Valette, with a request for boats to transport the garrison to Il Borgo; the Grand Master, they knew, would have confidence in that Knight's words. Coming to St. Angelo, de Medrano told of the fort's condition; pointed out that it could be held only by means of constant reinforcements, which was merely another way of draining the life-blood of the Order; and suggested that it would be better to bring the garrison back to St. Angelo, where the united strength of the Knights could make common cause against the infidel.

These arguments were presented at a council of the Grand Crosses, and when la Vallette asked an expression of opinion his hearers one and all agreed with de Medrano.

But the Grand Master was of a different mind.

"Our Heavenly Father knows," he said, "that I would not sacrifice uselessly the meanest creature on the island, much less my own Brethren in the Order. But it is imperative that St. Elmo be held to the uttermost. After our own strength, supported by God and St. John, all we have to rely on is the Sicilian succours, and Don Garcia has said that if

St. Elmo is in the hands of the Turks he will not risk the fleet of Spain in our behalf. The post must be held at all costs. The viceroy cannot desert us, and be assured that I will not desert the Brethren. All that is needed for the defence shall be supplied, and if necessary I will myself come and take over the command, to give heart to the faltering and to make good the walls or die in their defence."

With this reply, de Medrano went back to the fortress. He himself, with de Broglio, the Bailiff of Negropont, de Miranda, and some of the older Knights, professed themselves satisfied; they knew, they said, how lightly the Grand Master esteemed his own life in the balance with the cause of Christ; and they would shed the last drops of their blood in defence of the post assigned them. But some of the younger Brethren were not so easily reconciled. It was a wanton and useless waste of life, they said, to keep them there; none of them begrudged his life to the cause, but they would not tamely submit to be penned up like helpless sheep, awaiting the onslaught of the wolves; and since the Grand Master would not accede to their request and take them off, they would sally out against the infidel and die honorably in battle. A letter to this effect was drawn up and signed by fifty of the Knights, and, de Medrano refusing to carry it, the missive was entrusted to another of the Order, whom I will not name; he afterward repented of his error and found a glorious and honorable death in the final assault.

La Vallette read this letter with mingled sorrow and indignation.

"It is not enough for you to die," he told the messenger. "You must die in the manner which I command. At the time of your reception into the Order, you swore a solemn vow to obey me in all things. It is my judgment that St. Elmo be maintained to the end, and I call upon you for obedience to your oath.

"But that I may not seem to hold your remonstrances too light, I will send three good men to inspect St. Elmo and report whether or not, in their estimation, the fortress can be held. Also, I will despatch a galley to Sicily, to urge upon the viceroy the need of haste. Will this content you?"

The messenger said that it would, and the four returned together to St. Elmo, where they found the mutinous Knights already throwing the ammunition into the wells, that it might not be of assistance to the Turks, so sure they were of la Vallette's reply.

The emissaries were shown all over the works, and two of them agreed that the place was not tenable. But the third, the Chevalier Castriota, of the langue of Italy, dissented.

"The fortress is in bad state, I admit," he said. "But its condition is far from desperate. With fresh troops and supplies from Il Borgo, it may yet hold out for no little time. I think your fears are exaggerated, my brethren."

"By the Hand of St. John!" shouted one. "This touches my honor! I and my fellows say that it cannot be held. Would you give us the lie?" And he clapped hand to his hilt.

"Save your sword for the Paynim," answered Castriota, with a touch of contempt. "It is well known that in war private quarrels must give way to the public good. I will not fight you."

"You are bold enough with the skins of others," sneered one. "But sufficiently tender of your own."

This was too much for Castriota's southern blood, and his temper burst its bounds.

"By the living God!" he flared. "If you say that it is fear which keeps me from fighting, Sir François, you lie!" He glared about. "And I will say further, that none save a pack of cowards could have sent such a letter to the Grand Master. There are women in Il Borgo with stouter hearts than you!"

This was the signal for an instant uproar. Swords were drawn, and fifty challenges were flung at Castriota, who promptly accepted them en bloc. But the commander de Broglio and the Bailiff of Negropont kept their heads and to stop the tumult sent men to ring the alarm bell, thereby summoning each Knight to his own especial post.

Returning to St. Angelo, Castriota reported his findings to la Valette, and boldly offered to raise a force, cross to St. Elmo, and hold it against the Turks. To this la Vallette agreed, saying only:

"But the force must be of volunteers; no constraint may be used in such a case."

Volunteers pressed forward to offer themselves, Knights, mercenaries, and Maltese contending for the honor, and the Grand Master wrote at once to the rebellious Brethren.

"Your prayer is granted," he told them. "Volunteers are ready to take your place, and will be set across this very evening. Resign your post to them, my children, and return to St. Angelo. There you will be safe, and at the same time I shall be relieved from my fears for St. Elmo."

This reply struck the mutinous Knights with consternation. They had expected la Vallette to withdraw his forces to Il Borgo, abandoning St. Elmo altogether—indeed, such was their desire. Or, failing that, they were willing to sacrifice themselves in one mad onfall. But this—to have others replace them in the post with which they had been trusted— meant dishonor of the blackest. And no Knight of us all but could face the most dreadful death better than dishonor. The Bailiff of Negropont told me me, afterward, that the distress of the rebellious ones at this reply was pitiful indeed. Many of them weeping, they surrounded him and begged him to write for them to la Vallette; they avowed their penitence, and would obey the Grand Master implicitly if he would but relent and not disgrace them forever.

"It will be of no avail," the Bailiff told them. "I know Jehan Parisot de la Vallette too well to think that he will relent, when once his mind is fixed."

"But in any case, write," besought the spokesman. "By the Hand of St. John, this cannot be endured! I will fall on my sword rather than return in shame to St. Angelo!"

"And I! And I!" cried others, so in the end the Bailiff consented.

The letter was written, enclosed in oiled silk, and carried to la Vallette by a Maltese, who swam the harbor with the package tied about his neck. But it was coldly received by the Grand Master, who replied curtly, saying that insubordinate veterans were less to be depended on than new recruits who would obey.

At this the misery of the rebellious ones was indescribable. They wept aloud, tore their hair, beat their breasts, and called on Our Heavenly Father to spare them. And two were restrained from suicide only by force. In their distress they wrote again to la Vallette, most humbly beseeching his pardon, and vowing that if he would but overlook their fault they would give instant obedience to his lightest word.

And now the Grand Master yielded, feeling perhaps that it would not be well to push brave men to despair. He accordingly dismissed the volunteers, keeping only enough to replace the losses of the garrison, and sent these few across with food, ammunition, and supplies for repairing the works. I was one of those who went, and I can vouch for it that the delight of the former mutineers, on receiving permission to remain, was as boundless as their misery had been. In truth, the laughter and mirth and general rejoicing, the self-congratulation, verged on the hysterical—which is not altogether surprising, in view of the strain under which these men had been for some weeks past.

So behold me once more within the walls of St. Elmo, now sadly battered and wrecked from what they were when I was there before. But ere I relate what befell me there I must turn back in my narrative and tell of an incident which took place during the negotiations between the Grand Master and the mutineers, for this adventure not only brought me some small reputation, but had a distinct bearing on later events.

While de Miranda was making ready his expedition, David Evans came to my lodging, craving speech with me. Being admitted, he stood twisting his cap and trying to find words until at length I grew impatient.

"What is it?" I asked. "Speak out, man!"

"Sir Richard," he began, hesitatingly, "I have news which might be of interest to the Grand Master."

"Why not take it to him, then?"

"Well . . . well . . . I know you better . . . and, to speak plain, I am afeared of him."

"What cause have you to fear him? Have you been up to some mischief?"

"Faith, no! But he looks at one so . . . like a lion, as it were. And he has never married, so cannot feel for a poor fellow who—"

"Who has a wife or two wherever he sets foot," I finished, smiling.

He grinned shamefacedly.

"Faith, the dears are so charming, how can a man ignore them?"

"Especially your Muscovite spouse," I answered, dryly, recalling his description of her.

"She was perchance an error of judgment," he admitted. "We can all make mistakes. But you, Sir Richard, can speak with him face to face, and I thought . . ."

"So be it. Your news?"

But still he fussed with his cap and looked uneasily about, until I bade him:

"Go on, chew. I can see your restlessness without it."

"Thank you, Sir Richard. By your leave——" And he loaded his mouth with the aromatic weed. "When one is used to it he feels its loss. For my news, then, it is this.

"While guarding a party of our galley-slaves as they washed in the Bay of Vermin, I chanced to overhear two of them conversing. The black followers of Mahound knew not that I understand their language, so they spoke freely, and I learned that Mustapha is planning a secret attack on St. Angelo."

"Rest easy; he will not take us unaware. You know the castle bears, carved in the stone above the gate, an eye, an ear, and a goose, typifying the eternal vigilance of the guardians."

"The eye and the ear I can understand, as emblems of watchfulness, but why the goose, Sir Richard? That is beyond my simple wit."

"In allusion to the Roman geese who cackled and so gave warning of a camisado by the Gauls, thus saving the Capitol."

"By Our Lady, a wise conceit! But, by your leave, this is a different matter. Through a traitor within the walls, working hand in glove with a renegado in the Moslem camp, the foul Paynim have learned of the catacombs which undermine the

island. They plan to set their men ashore at Ras
Hanzier, thence to make their way underground to
the crypt beneath the Church of St. Lawrence, and
when the Knights are resting they will creep out,
slay the sentries, and throw open the gates. At the
same time, an attack launched on our outer defences
will try to smash through and win the gates. It is
for to-morrow night, they said. At least, from what
I heard, I take it that this was concerted with one
of the garrison, though it may be the renegado's
own invention."

"I am loath," I told him, "to credit such villainy
of any within the walls. Still," I acknowledged, "it
may be true, and in any case your news is of utmost
import. The Grand Master shall know of it at
once. How many will be in the party?"

"I cannot say for sure. About fifty, I think.
They will not need many to open the gates—they
are trusting to surprise—and a large number would
hamper one another."

"True. You have done well, David, and shall be
duly thanked."

Still he hesitated, seeming to have more to say,
and I told him:

"Speak! Never boggle over your words."

"If a party be sent to meet the dogs in the catacombs, may I be of it?"

"You like underground fighting?"

"I hate it," he rejoined, frankly. "But I hate the Moslem worse. And if they are to be taken unaware—"

"Be content; I will do what I can for you."

He thanked me and withdrew, and I hastened to la Vallette with the tale.

"And," I begged, "if a party is sent to cut them off, may I not volunteer for the service?"

"You know the passages well, Sir Richard?" the Grand Master inquired.

"I cannot lay claim to know their vast extent completely," I replied. "But I have some knowledge of them. During our leisure time last winter, the Chevalier de la Mara and I spent many hours exploring them, taking torches and a clue of thread such as Ariadne gave Theseus when he invaded the Cretan labyrinth of King Minos, to slay the Minotaur."

"A sage precaution, that," he approved, nodding. "Would it be better, think you, to lie in wait for them in the catacombs, or when they come ashore at Ras Hanzier?"

"Under favor, sir, in the catacombs, just before they come to the crypt of St. Lawrence. They will be alert while landing, but having come so far without molestation, they will have relaxed their caution somewhat. Also, in the catacombs they will be on unfamiliar ground, and their superstitious souls will be oppressed, so they may the more readily be thrown into panic."

Again the Grand Master nodded.

"It is well thought of," he agreed. "We will take care of them."

"And I may be of the party?"

"Better yet," he smiled. "You shall lead it." I must have shown my delight, for he added: "That pleases you?"

"I am honored, sir. Beyond my deserts, I fear."

"I think there is but little danger of your failing to acquit yourself creditably, Sir Richard. How many will you take?"

"Fifty should be ample, since we are taking them by surprise. Ten arquebusiers, ten with hand-bombs, and the rest men-at-arms. And I doubt not that by the aid of God and St. John we can give the infidels a lesson which will discourage like attempts in future. May I take de la Mara with me? He would regret to miss such an enterprise."

"Certainly," la Vallette granted. "Well, make your dispositions. Sir Oliver will give you an order for the men and supplies that you require. And God speed you well!"

Finding Juan, I told him of the plan, whereat he laughed aloud in sheer delight.

"Ever in luck's way, Ricardo mio," he said. "Por Dios! We should be able to teach them a

goodly lesson, as you say. They may learn that
there is no road so smooth but one may stumble on it.
I forgive you for dragging me into your poisoning
expedition. Where will you place your ambuscado?"

"In the long, straight passage just before reaching the crypt. We will erect a barricade across it,
lie in wait behind this breastwork, and have half our
party lurking in the cross-passage that branches off
a hundred paces down, to take them in the rear."

He approved, and we set about choosing the men.

Selecting fifty of the stoutest, I addressed a few
words to them, telling of the enterprise and warning
them to secrecy, then set them to making hand-
bombs, five for each of my bombers. This done,
I withdrew them from duty, and bade them spend
the next twenty-four hours in rest.

"And," I assured them, "I promise faithfully, by
my knightly honor, to hang any of you who gets
drunk or who babbles a word of our project." Happily, however, no occasion arose for such drastic
measures.

The intervening time, before we set out, I passed
in reviewing my plans, discussing them with Juan,
and in going with him to say farewell to Lady
Madeleine and the Countess de Zerafa. Of course
we told them nothing of our immediate project, but
they knew that I expected to return to St. Elmo, so

the visit and the adieus were not out of place. The
ladies were most gracious, chatting pleasantly with
us and wishing me the best of fortune, and when we
left it seemed that the Lady Madeleine held my
hand a trifle longer than strict courtesy demanded,
and looked a bit wistfully into my eyes. Still, what
if she did? We were excellent friends, and I had
saved her from a most dismal fate. Also, she had
cared for me when I was wounded, and everyone
knows that the surest way to gain a liking for anyone is to do something for him. I said as much to
Juan, and he snorted.

"'Liking'!" he said. "A man with half an eye
could see that she is over head and ears in love with
you, Ricardo. That is, anyone save yourself could
see it. Yes, laugh! Go on, now, laugh some more.
The Holy Virgin deliver me from falling in love
with a fish-blooded English damsel! Must one build
a fire under you, as my countrymen do with a balk-
ing mule? Though I am fain to admit that you are
ready enough when it comes to fighting."

"You forget," I told him, "that I am betrothed
in England. Or as good as betrothed. My honor
is engaged."

"So it is, so it is," he sighed. "For myself, I
should consider a bird in the hand worth two in the
bush."

"Nay, one real bird in the bush may well outweigh

an imaginary one in the hand. The Lady Madeleine
has perchance some liking for me, but as to love—
you have read too many romances of chivalry,
Juan."

"Well, well, I shall, I perceive, build a fire under
you yet. Now of this affair. How will you divide
the party?" And so the subject was changed.

I gave my men careful instructions, saw that they
were well fed, inspected their arms, had them all
duly shriven, led them into the church, down to the
crypt, and so to the catacombs.

After leaving the crypt, we made our way for a
hundred paces or so along the passage, which here
was wide enough for five men to walk abreast. The
floor sloped gently downward, and our torches
showed that many pieces of rock lay scattered
about, either fallen from the roof or left by the
workmen who dug the place. I bade my men gather
a quantity of these and erect a barricade across the
passage, to the height of a man's chest, and half the
party, including all the arquebusiers and bombers,
lay down behind it. The remaining twenty-five I
placed under command of de la Mara, sending them
another hundred paces along the tunnel, to where
a smaller passage branched off nearly at right angles
to the main one. This smaller tunnel was a blind
alley, and had in past times been used as a place of
burial, so that now it contained great quantities of

bones. The flanking party would wait here until my arquebusiers had done their work, when they would sally out and fall on the rear of the Turks at the same time that I assailed them in front.

The bombers were in charge of Evans, who had spent the afternoon instructing them, and altogether I was very well satisfied with the arrangements; the Turks, if all went as I anticipated, were due for a most unpleasant surprise. I took particular pains to give the barricade an accidental appearance, saw to it that each man of my party had one good drink of wine and no more, and noted with gratification that the expected gentle current of air was blowing up the tunnel against our faces, so that it would carry off the smoke of our slow matches and not betray us by the smell. Then I ordered all matches lighted and torches extinguished, and lay down to await the invaders.

A quarter of a mile or so from where we were our tunnel joined another, this latter following an irregular course through many windings and branches to distant Ras Hanzier, some miles away. Removing my burgonet, that its gleam might not betray me, I took my post, standing erect behind the barricade and watching for the appearance of the Turks. I had enjoined quiet on my men, but now as they lay on the floor I could hear their heavy breathing, which might not be completely silenced. Still, it was not enough to betray us, and at least there was no talking. Looking back, I could see the glow of the matches, now and then gleaming brighter as the men blew on them to keep them alight, and I passed the word back that all matches must be hidden; the rocky walls and roof were damp with moisture, and the reflection might be seen.

It was a strange experience, and far from pleasant, waiting thus cooped in the bowels of the earth for death to come stalking toward us from the dark. We were too far below ground to hear the thunder of the guns, but we could feel the stone beneath us shake from the concussion as the vibrations carried along the solid rock on which the island is founded. The quivering was constant, uninterrupted, though from time to time a heavier tremble told me that one of the huge basilicas had been fired. I felt a peculiar and vastly disagreeable sensation in my throat, a choking or stifling, as though I could not draw my breath; I seemed to be buried under tons and tons of rock which pressed down on my bosom, so that I was slowly suffocating. But this, I told myself, was folly; I must not yield to it; the road lay open behind me to the upper air, and the breeze in my face was cool and fresh, even if slightly damp. So I shook myself, put the thought from me, and returned to my vigil.

We had about an hour to wait, but at length I

saw some pin-points of light far in the distance, and I whispered to Evans, who lay behind me:

"Make ready; they are coming."

He sent the message along, and I could hear faint sounds as the men gathered themselves together. I crouched down so that only my eyes were above the rampart, and watched as the Turks drew near, their loose, voluminous, and light-colored garments making it easy to follow their progress. When they were a little past the mouth of the side tunnel I drew down completely out of sight, to trace their approach by ear. On they came, until some fifteen paces from us, when they halted and began chattering excitedly. Evans moved close to me and breathed softly:

"They were not expecting our barrier . . . they dread an ambuscado . . . nay, it is all right; they are coming on."

Nearer and nearer came the footsteps, the flicker of the torches, until I judged that they were well-nigh upon us, when I snapped my fingers and the bombers lit their fuses. At that instant a torch was thrust over the barricade and a black-bearded Turk stared full in my face, his eyes wide with amazement.

"Allah!" he burst out, to fall before my sword-thrust even as the first bombs, with shattering roar, drowned his exclamation.

The other bombs followed in a shower, bursting with terrific noise in that pent-up place, the sound magnified a hundred-fold as it echoed and reëchoed from the walls of rock. Howls and screams of agony mingled with shouts of terror as the invaders turned to flee, trampling one another in their frantic desire to escape.

"Allah! Allah!" they yelled, calling on the name of their god, and others cried aloud:

"Djinn! Djinn!" Which meant, Juan told me later, that they took us for demons.

In the confusion, some of their garments took fire from the torches or from the bombs, and this added to their pain and fright, so that within a dozen breaths the whole troop was in utter panic. Before they could gather themselves into order, before they could make any kind of retreat, our bombs were flung, and I shouted:

"Arquebusiers!"

The musketeers rose and poured a volley into the milling crowd, following it with two more volleys from their pistols, and then, sword in hand, I scrambled over the barricade, shouting to my men:

"Charge! St. John! St. John!"

My troopers followed, eager to come to grips with the infidel, and hearing my call, Juan swept out at the head of his men from ambuscade, shouting the war-cry of Spain:

"St. Iago y cierra, España!"

The Turks, caught between two forces, were quickly ended. They fought back, to be sure, as a trapped rat will fight a terrier, but to as little purpose, and we cut them down to the last man. I tried to take some prisoners, that we might question them, but there was no restraining the islanders; a Maltese hates a Turk worse than he hates the Father of Evil, and their blood was up. The only captives we took were wounded men, and they proved too far gone to answer our questions. I had hoped to learn the name of the traitor within our walls, if such there was, but the only one who knew, so far as we could tell, was the renegado, and he was killed by a bomb. So we were obliged to return without discovering that; still, we had done some damage, and hoped to discourage future like attempts.

None of my men was even wounded, save that one bomber had taken a slight cut on the left arm from a scimitar. This Evans bound up, placing on the wound a well-chewed mass of his Indian herb, which he declared to be a sovereign remedy for all such injuries. For myself, as by torchlight I looked about on the scene of carnage, with the blood, the scattered bodies, many of them frightfully mangled by our bombs, and the reek of sulphur and burning cloth, I was violently sick, and must lean against the wall to regain my strength. But

presently recovering, I summoned my men from
their task of looting the slain, and we marched back
to our quarters. And glad I was to see once more
the dark blue sky above me, with its twinkling stars,
to breathe deep the clear air, to hear the rolling
thunder of the guns.

Dismissing my men, I went directly to report to
la Vallette. He heard me out, was graciously
pleased to approve me, and said:

"To-morrow I will have built two walls, each
twenty feet thick, enclosing between them your field
of battle. Thus shall we halt any such future attempts before they are a menace, and at the same
time prevent word of this affair getting to the Turks.
If we can keep the fate of this expedition a mystery
it will work on their superstitious minds, to discourage them from another essay. You will caution
your men against talking of it, Sir Richard."

"According to command," I acknowledged, then
asked: "The assault on the gate was repulsed?"

"It was, without much difficulty. Though had we
not been warned, or had there been fifty resolute
men of Islam within our walls, the tale might well
be different. Now rest, that you may be fresh to
go with the reinforcements to St. Elmo."

"When do they leave?" I inquired.

"I am sending some troops to-morrow night, directly after compline."

"I will be ready. And I thank you most heartily for granting me to-night's expedition."

He smiled.

"I am sure it was a great favor," he replied, jestingly. "Doubtless you feel that I am being most gracious in permitting you to risk death in St. Elmo?"

"It is not the risk of death that is the favor," I answered, "but the chance of honor."

"Bravely spoken, Sir Richard." And rising, he laid his hand on my shoulder. "Were all the Brethren as stout of heart as you, I should have no fear of the outcome. You may retire now."

And bowing deeply, I withdrew, much heartened by this praise from our revered and gallant leader. Truly, he knew well the value of a word spoken in due season!

CHAPTER VI

Of the Death of Dragut; and the Last Days of St. Elmo

IN spite of Dragut's counsel, the Turks had not yet completely invested St. Elmo, and it was still possible for us to set men and supplies across the Grand Harbor. Later, when the great corsair's insistence had taken effect, the lines were closely drawn, and St. Elmo was cut off from aid, but at this time the passage was open. The Turks had sentinels along the water-front, it is true, but a lack of vigilance is characteristic of the infidel, so by the use of a moderate amount of care we could elude them. This indifferent watchfulness has ever been a source of amazement to me, both during the siege of Malta and since then, so that many times I have had occasion to thank God that He has blinded the Paynim eyes.

So it was that on the fifteenth of June, about ten in the evening, I set out from St. Angelo to make my way into the besieged fortress. La Vallette had changed his plan of sending reinforcements, since these were not yet needed, so two Maltese sailors rowed me across in a small boat, and as I sat idle in the stern and looked about I thought how strangely man's work was at variance with Nature's. It was a calm and peaceful evening, with overhead a clear blue sky, the west tinged with the glowing colors of sunset, and all around us lay the quiet sea, intensely blue, moving only in gentle swells. All the scene breathed of peace and sweetness, while a scant half mile away men were tearing one another with steel and iron and stone, blasting one another out of life with villainous saltpetre, slaughtering one another, dying in agony, and all in the name of God. How far had we wandered from the teachings of the gentle and pitiful Christ, to be doing such things in His name! To be sure, we were attacked, and it was right for us to defend the true faith—but how if, perchance, Islam were the true faith, Allah the true God, Mohammed His prophet? Certainly these Moslems insisted that they were right, and as strongly as we insisted on our God. Suddenly, with a thrill of horror, I realized where my thoughts had led me, and I crossed myself, bent my head, and silently asked forgiveness for my sin. None the less, I could not help feeling it a pity that the Turks would not accept Christ, that all this suffering might be spared.

It was no difficult task to make my way to the underground passage, and once within the citadel,

I reported straight to the commander, the Chevalier de Broglio, who gave me warm welcome.

"In truth," said he, "you are come at a good time, Sir Richard. The bombardment has been fierce beyond measure to-day, and it is my belief that a general assault is being prepared for the morrow. But by the grace of Our Heavenly Father, and with the aid of good St. John, I doubt not that we shall be able to thrust them back, as heretofore."

I needed no one to tell me that the bombardment had been extraordinarily savage; my own ears had informed me of that fact. But coming up from the underground passage within the confines of St. Elmo, I had not been able to judge the effects of the gun-fire, so now I asked de Broglio's permission to go outside the citadel and look around.

"By all means do so," he granted, readily. "The infidels have gnawed a breach on our southern ramparts, and it will probably be there that they will deliver their assault. You should familiarize yourself with our defences, but be not rash, Sir Richard; do not expose yourself without due cause."

I promised, and sallied out, almost at once meeting the younger la Vallette, with his shadow, Polastra. The former was a handsome youth of about my own age—perhaps a year or two younger—straight, tall, dark, and with a grave look not unbecoming in one whose heritage was of the nobility and poesy of Languedoc. I liked him vastly, but it seemed to me foolish in him to affect gilded armor; it made him too conspicuous a mark, and, indeed, proved fatal ere the siege was ended. Polastra was of the Italian langue, and the very antithesis of his friend, being short, stoutly built, and not good-looking, albeit he owned a frank, attractive manner which caused one to forget the homeliness of his features. The two gave me greeting, and volunteered to show me around.

"You will find things changed since your former visit, Sir Richard," said la Vallette. "We have lost the ravelin and the counterscarp, with all the outworks, so that we now hold but the castle itself. And the Turks have effected a breach there as well, so that we expect an assault in force to-morrow. However, by God's grace, we shall make good our stand."

We went first to the breach, and I was shocked at the gaping hole which had been torn in the wall; it was wide enough for twenty men to come through abreast, and the dry moat outside was so choked with fallen masonry, pieces of rock, and cannon-balls as to furnish no defence at all—the Turks could scramble directly over the litter. The wall was forty feet thick and sixty or seventy in height, and I had thought it impregnable, but now I must grant that Messer Cassar had been right; a mountain of adamant could not withstand those terrible guns. And they were still thundering, those guns, their shot and shell ever pounding our devoted ramparts, and with the roar of cannon-fire there mingled the shattering impact of the bullets, the hissing and smash of exploding bombs, and now and then a crash as with a cloud of dust some loosened section of masonry toppled and fell in ruin. Over all hung a dense and sulphurous cloud that reeked of the Pit, and through this, as from time to time it thinned before a breeze, we could see the flashes of the guns, or could make out some projectile hurtling toward us through the air. One such came flying through the breach, glanced from a fragment of rock, and bounded and rolled to our very feet. It was a bomb, as we could tell from its sputtering fuse, and with one impulse we three flung ourselves upon it. Polastra reached it first, and plucked out the fuse just in time, for there was less than an inch left. The Chevalier de Medrano happened to be passing, and he laughed and waved his hand when the young Italian held up the remnant of fuse between thumb and finger.

"Close work, mon brave!" he called. "Felicitations!" And he passed on.

If I had been shocked at the appearance of the walls, I was still more shocked at the aspect of the defenders. One and all, Knights, mercenaries, and volunteers, they showed the effect of the long strain, the many vigils, the endless peril, the unceasing watchfulness. Drawn, haggard, and weary, many of them with bandaged wounds and all with armor dented, with clothing stained, to the casual glance they seemed at the last extremity of their powers. But every one of them showed in the set of his mouth and the proud carriage of his head a fierce, indomitable courage. Men passed us with lagging feet, too worn to step out briskly, but by sheer strength of will they held their heads erect and looked about with unfaltering eyes. By the Hand of St. John, I was glad to be of that gallant company!

That night, after the evening meal, those of the Knights who were not on duty gathered in the little chapel, scarce twenty by forty feet, and there received the Most Blessed Sacrament from the hands of Brother Jehan, an ecclesiastic of the langue of France. Then we knelt on the stones while he offered prayer, and with him we repeated three noble psalms: "Domine, quid multiplicati sunt qui tribulant me," "Dominus regit me, et nihil mihi deerit," and that glorious one which says: "Deus noster refugium et virtus, adjutor in tribulationibus quae invenierunt non nimis. Propterea non timiebimus dum turbabitur terra et transferentur montes in cor maris." *

* Psalms iii, xxiii, and xlvi.

Then Brother Jehan asked the blessing of Heaven on the defenders of Christ, and with resolute and uplifted spirits we went to rest.

For myself, I could not sleep. It was plain from what I had seen that St. Elmo was nearing its end; that our last days were at hand. One or two more assaults, a little more battering from the guns, and the horde of Islam would roll over us as the incoming tide sweeps over a rock—but when the flood should recede we would no longer be there. I hoped that my friends in England would learn how well I had died, and I rejoiced, for the first time, that my father and mother were not living; they would not mourn my loss, and I could look forward to meeting them again ere long. I tossed and turned from side to side, trying to rest, until at length, some time after midnight, I rose, set up my sword in a ray of moonlight and knelt before the cross of its hilt, praying fervently for strength to meet whatever might come. To take one's chance in the rush and excitement of battle is no such great matter, but it is far from easy to sit and watch certain death approach on lagging feet. At length, somewhat eased, I lay down and fell into a half slumber, through which I still heard the unceasing thunder of the guns. In my dreams Lady Madeleine came to my side, holding a crucifix before me and exhorting me to be of stout heart, and I recall wondering why

I should dream of her rather than of Lady Alice,
but before I could solve this problem young la Vallette came to my chamber and roused me.

"Up, Sir Richard!" he said. "It is near dawn,
and the cannon-fire slackens. We must be in the
breach at earliest light."

I had merely taken off my burgonet, cuirass, and
boots to lie down, so it was the work of a moment
to dress and gird on my sword. Going to the refec-
tory, I found most of the Knights there, and bread
and wine were served to us, which we ate hastily,
each one as he finished going to his post. I had been
assigned a place in the breach, with la Vallette, Polastra, and a number of others, and we hurried
thither, reporting to de Medrano, who commanded
there.

Presently the sun rose in unclouded glory, the infidel guns entirely ceased their growling, and we
could see the dark clouds of attackers gathering in
their trenches. The Ottoman fleet had moved
around into the Grand Harbor, and was bombard-
ing St. Elmo on that side, but this was a matter of
no present concern. Also, a body of Turks was
forming for an escalade against the northern part
of the wall, but we were confident that the Bailiff
of Negropont would care for them; the defenders
there were well provided with logs and stones and
molten lead to hurl on the ladders, and with that

implement which the Turks dreaded most of all, the fire-hoop. This was the invention of the Chevalier Ramon Fortuny, of the langue of Castile, and consisted of a metal hoop some four feet across, wound with rags which had been soaked in bitumen and nitre. Setting these alight, the defenders would drop them over the heads of the assailants, like a child playing at ring-toss, and the flowing garments of the Turks insured an agonizing death for any thus ringed. No, it was at the breach that lay the chief danger to St. Elmo.

And the Turks realized this, for they had set a body of at least four thousand arquebusiers to sweep our ramparts with bullets, and they were sending against us the very flower of the Ottoman Empire, that body of savage fighters known as the Yeni-Tscheri. Marching out from their trenches, these formed in column, advancing rapidly up the slope to the castle, and seeming, with their close-packed line of fur caps, like some dark, rippling river. Since we were on the southern side of St. Elmo, the guns of St. Angelo, across the harbor, were brought to bear at a scant half mile, and did great execution among the charging columns. Our own cannon also tore great holes in the ranks of the Yeni-Tscheri, and hundreds of them fell before the fire of our arquebusiers. But on they came and on, while we within the breach drew our swords, set our teeth, and made ready, hundreds against thousands, to hold our place for the greater glory of God and the salvation of Christendom.

On and on, up the slope, across the rock-filled ditch, the survivors pressed over the bodies of the fallen, right up against our wall. Scimitars flashed in the sun, bullets sang all about, white teeth gleamed in dark faces as the worshippers of Mahound shouted their war-cry:

"Allaho akbar! Allaho akbar!"

And we raised our shout in defiance:

"St. John! St. John!"

I was in the front rank of the defenders, with de Medrano, de Miranda, young la Vallette, Polastra, and a crowd of mercenaries and volunteers, and just as the Yeni-Tscheri reached our wall a cloud of gun-smoke swept across and hid them from our view. But they burst through this, a savage horde, and with shouts and yells and clash of steel the battle joined.

I have no clear recollection of the fight. It was a furious whirl of bodies, cut and slash and stab of weapons, crackling fire of musketry, stench of gun-smoke stinging the nostrils and choking both Christian and Moslem alike. Faces, brown and bearded, came and went; fierce dark eyes glowed at me and disappeared; shrieks and groans and yells and shouts resounded in my ears; I trod on bodies that writhed and twisted or lay still; and ever I warded or struck or stabbed. A giant whom I recognized as Yussef, captor of Lady Madeleine, beat down my guard and, cursing furiously, raised his scimitar to finish me. I noticed the plaster that bound his jaws, and wondered at the fortitude of the man, fighting with such an injury. But as he started the downward stroke a pistol roared in my ear and Yussef's face vanished, to be instantly replaced by another. I finished this man and turned to see who had saved me—barely in time, for it was Xuereb beside me, and a Turk had engaged him in front, while another was stabbing at him from the rear. I drove my sword through the latter's forearm, and as he dropped his scimitar I thrust him through the body, thus paying my debt. Xuereb got past the other's guard and ended his fighting days.

After a time the battle slackened somewhat, for both Christian and Moslem grew weary, and as by agreement we drew back to rest and take breath. The arquebus-fire also slackened, and during this pause a daring Turk managed to scramble up the shattered wall and plant the standard of the Crescent on our rampart.

"Allaho akbar!" he shouted, and again: "Allaho akbar!"

An answering shout of triumph went up from the horde of Islam, and a howl of execration from the

IT WAS A BEAUTIFUL FIGHT.

Christian host. Like a mountain goat, de Medrano went springing up the ruins, and by common consent we all, defender and attacker alike, turned to watch the duel. It was a beautiful fight, for both were expert swordsmen, and we thrilled at the play of steel. Back and forth they fought, round and round, their blades twisting, advancing, recoiling, writhing like snakes, in feint, thrust, guard, riposte. At length de Medrano lunged quickly, his sword passed through the other's body, and the Moslem staggered, dropped his scimitar, spread his arms wide, and fell from the rampart, turning over and over in his fall. And now it was our turn to utter a joyous and triumphant shout, while the Moslems shrieked in fury as de Medrano wrenched loose the staff and cast the banner to the fosse outside the wall. But even as he did so he tottered, clasped his hand to his breast, and sank on the rampart. The men on the wall rushed to lift him, but an arquebus ball had smashed through his corselet and pierced his heart. Thus passed a very gallant gentleman. And with that the battle joined once more.

While we were fighting in the breach, de Broglio and the Bailiff of Negropont were beating off the escalade against the northern wall, and a storming party which essayed the southern wall was well-nigh wholly destroyed by the guns of St. Angelo, with those of St. Michael aiding. But during the

battle a most serious disaster befell us, greatly
heartening the attackers. This was when a bomb—
some said from one of the guns of la Sangle
—landed in the midst of our ammunition magazine.
We were stunned by a sudden roar so titanic that it
dwarfed all other sounds, and the solid rock heaved
and shook beneath our feet as from an earthquake.
Turning, I saw a vast black cloud rise above St.
Elmo, then spread out and settle like a dark canopy
over the island, shutting out the light of the sun
as might a storm. For a moment the combat was
stilled, while both Turk and Christian gazed in
wonder, then the Moslems, taking heart, rushed
on us with new ferocity. But far from being dis-
mayed by this evil stroke of fate, our men gathered
themselves, doubled their efforts, and pressed the
attackers so fiercely that the Yeni-Tscheri, whose
proud boast it was that they had never retreated
from a fight, were driven from the breach and
hurled back down the slope. Hand to hand and
breast to breast, mingled in one confused mass, too
tightly packed to use our swords, we fought with
tooth and fist and dagger, driving the Moslems
from our sacred ground.

For hours the fight raged, until the sun stood
overhead, its tropic heat burning attacker and defender alike. Our throats were parched, our
tongues swollen from thirst, but still we would not

yield, and still we thrust back charge after charge. At length, about noon, Mustapha saw that the castle was not to be won, and that the Yeni-Tscheri could scarcely be brought again to the assault, so he bade the trumpets sound the recall, and the Moslem forces sullenly drew off, while our men galled their retreat with cannon and with arquebus. And as they went we raised a cheer of exultation which was answered across the water from St. Michael and St. Angelo.

But the victory was a costly one. None of us all was without one or more wounds, while of the Order, sixteen Knights besides de Medrano had fallen, and of the common soldiers three hundred. And here let me pay deserved tribute to these last, for though of common blood they fought as stoutly and as gallantly throughout as any who could show his quarterings of nobility. Indeed, one of the Maltese volunteers, Hercules Xerri by name, displayed such conspicuous valor that, being returned to St. Angelo with a mortal wound, he was knighted before death by the Grand Master, in order that his family might be forever ennobled.

Happily, the Turks relaxed their vigilance in the Grand Harbor, so we were not obliged to use the underground pass to communicate with St. Angelo, but could make our way out through the breach, down to the water, and so across in boats. And all that night, barges and skiffs were plying to and fro, taking our seriously wounded to the town and bringing replacements of men and stores. And so eager were the men of St. Angelo to join us in the post of death that la Vallette was obliged to refuse twelve Knights of the Italian langue, since our number was complete.

One of our most seriously wounded was the Bailiff of Negropont, but he refused to be sent back, and when la Vallette urged him to let a substitute take his place, the Bailiff replied that he would obey if ordered to do so, but he prayed the Grand Master to let him remain and die in defence of the true faith. The prayer was granted, and, needless to say, the more despondent among us were vastly stiffened in their courage by the incident; who could prove recreant, or flinch from danger, with so heroic an example before him?

By now we had begun to despair of receiving the promised aid from Sicily; surely if the viceroy had meant to come to our relief he would have been at Malta by now. The Knights spoke often of this, and could Don Garcia have heard the curses they bestowed on him, of a surety his sleep would have been disturbed for many a long month. The Chevalier de la Cerda was particularly bitter.

"It is not that I specially mind dying," he said, "for death comes to every man, and leaves us all on one level in the grave. But to die like a rat in a trap, while that swag-bellied, wine-bibbing coward sits idly by, he who could save us by stretching out his hand—that is what hurts."

"Let that flea stick in the wall," I told him, using a vulgar phrase. "We are vowed to fight the infidel, and are not like to have a better chance. You should be content, my friend."

Those who heard us laughed and applauded my words, and from then on there was less cursing of Don Garcia.

The seventeenth of June—that is, the day after the assault—was devoted by the Turks to completing the investment. It had finally penetrated their dull minds that St. Elmo was not to be reduced while men and stores could reach us from Il Borgo, and they had made a systematic hunt for the mouth of the underground way, blocking it, when found, with great piles of stone. A prisoner whom we took and questioned told us that Mustapha wished to send a detachment through to take us in the rear, but the utter vanishment of the party that Juan and I destroyed had so worked on the superstitious minds of the soldiers that they flatly refused to go. So a double good came of our little affair in the catacombs.

But Dragut insisted that the lines of investment be carried down to the very edge of the Grand Harbor, and this was done, a battery of heavy guns being mounted to command the water. Also, a company of arquebusiers was planted to sweep the landing-place, and the Turkish galleys held themselves in readiness to intercept any boats that might put out from Il Borgo. De Broglio sent a Maltese to carry word to la Vallette of our desperate condition, and this man, taking the water from our southern wall, swam for long stretches beneath the surface, at length reaching St. Angelo untouched by the bullets. The Grand Master at once loaded five barges with men and stores and sent them to our aid, but they might not force the passage; indeed, so prompt were the Turks that our would-be relief narrowly escaped destruction, and perforce returned whence they came. And seeing this, none of us could doubt that our end was near at hand.

During five days the Moslems made no assault, but harassed us with gun-fire, to widen the breach in our walls and wear down our men by long-continued strain. No small number of us were struck by bullets or wounded by exploding bombs, and among these were de la Cerda and a Knight of the langue of Aragon, whose name I have forgotten. An arquebus ball struck down the former while he was directing repairs to the wall, and as for the latter, a bomb burst squarely under his feet, so that all we found of him was the hilt of his sword and a fragment of his cuirass. But during these trying days one comfort was granted to us, and to me in particular, this grace coming about in the following manner.

Of course, we maintained a constant fire from our guns upon the besiegers, and one day while I was talking with the Chevalier de Guiral, who commanded our artillery, he asked me if I would like to try a shot with a culverin which was in action near us.

"But I know nothing of firearms," I objected, to which he answered:

"That need not hinder. Aim and fire it as best you may; you can scarce fail to produce some good effect."

I demurred a trifle more, but finally accepted, and the gunners charged the piece for me. I sighted along the top as I had seen the chief gunner do, and my eye was caught by a group of Paynim officers who were directing the placing of the seaward battery. I ordered the gun crew to swing the piece slightly, which they did, I aiming the while, and I then took the slow match from the chief gunner and laid it to the touch-hole. The cannon leaped and roared, belching forth a huge cloud of smoke, and de Guiral, who had stood to one side that he might observe my fortune, cried out with delight.

"Ha, an excellent shot, Sir Richard! By Our

Lady of Rocamadour, I will make you my chief gunner if you will take the post."

"How now?" I asked, peering at my target as the smoke blew aside. "What luck?"

"Impossible to better it," he assured me. "The ball struck fair in the midst of the group, sent three of the base infidels straight to hell, dismounted a gun, and glancing from that, broke off a splinter of rock which smote down another, either dead or wounded. And I think . . . yes . . . no . . . they are lifting him—yes, pardieu, it is Dragut himself!" He flung his arms around my neck and kissed me on both cheeks. "Ami de mon coeur, we are friends for life!"

I tried to look modest, but it is useless to deny that I was pleased.

"Nay," I said, deprecatingly, "it was but novice's luck."

"Luck or no luck, it was an excellent shot. Wait till de Broglio hears of this; it will cheer him vastly!"

De Guiral spread the news through the garrison, and I received many congratulations, which I accepted as becomingly as I might. We learned afterward that Dragut was not killed out of hand, but lingered in great pain for a week or more, until death put an end to his suffering. At least, though, he was in no condition to take any further part in the siege.

The twentieth of the month was the Feast of the Body of Our Lord, always celebrated with great pomp by the Order, and those in St. Angelo and Il Borgo observed it as usual, with a procession of Knights, together with the men and women of the town, ending with a High Mass in the Church of St. Lawrence. As for us, we had small heart for celebration, but all day long Brother Jehan kept his place before the altar in our little chapel, whither we repaired as opportunity offered, repeating prayers and partaking of the Blessed Sacrament.

That evening, as I was preparing for rest, a messenger was announced, and on being admitted he proved to be a Maltese, still dripping from his swim across the harbor. Saluting, he said:

"I begged the Grand Master to let me try my luck at eluding the black Paynim, that I might have a share in the fighting. He granted my request, and here I am. But a certain lady, hearing of my plan, gave me this packet for you, Sir Richard." And he handed me a small package wrapped in oiled silk.

Opening it, I found therein no word, but a single red rose, its stem thrust through a circlet of gold which I had often seen on Lady Madeleine's finger. Judge if it heartened me!

"If we come alive out of this pass," I told the man, "you shall have a rich reward, I pledge you my knightly word."

"I ask no reward," he answered, simply. "The lady granted me to kiss her hand. Have I your permission to withdraw?"

I nodded, unable to speak. But I am glad to say that I did reward him. He survived the siege, though crippled by wounds and unable to work, and I saw to it that he and his family had enough to keep them in comfort on their farm near Città Notable.

During the twenty-first of June, the fire of the besiegers was redoubled, opening new breaches and in places demolishing our wall utterly, even to the naked rock on which it was founded. Nor could we reply to it properly, for our ammunition was running low, so that the Turkish pioneers advanced in face of our weakened musketry, filling the whole length of the dry ditch with fascines, and covering these with damp earth, to prevent our burning them. A succession of false alarms kept us at our posts all that night, and with the dawn a general assault was launched against our walls.

This attack was more savage than the previous one, but fierce though it was, our defense was fiercer yet. Past all hope, our only thought was to sell our lives as dearly as possible, and we met the infidel with a savagery which outdid their devil-inspired rage. Hand to hand we fought, grappling in desperate encounter, until the ruins on which we stood were slippery with blood and piled with the bodies of the slain, of Christian and unbeliever mingled in one inextricable mass. Three times that vast horde came streaming up to our walls, brandishing their weapons and shouting their war-cries, and three times we met them and flung them back, until in despair they withdrew, and the evening sun saw the white cross of St. John still flying over the battered castle of St. Elmo.

But we could not withstand another assault, and it remained only to prepare for the inevitable doom which now hung over us. All that night, those who were able spent the long hours in bringing such comfort as we might to the wounded and dying, though in truth there was little we could do save carry water to men parched with fever and speak what words of cheer we might find. And stoutest of all in their high spirit were the Bailiff of Negro-pont and the Chevalier de Miranda, who though themselves sore wounded, proved a very tower of strength and comfort to the suffering ones, "as the shadow of a great rock in a weary land."

When morning came we embraced one another, saying farewell as became men about to die, yet not despairingly, buoyed up by the certainty of a glorious resurrection. Then we took in our arms those who were unable to stand but who could still wield a sword, and bore them to their posts, that they might strike a last blow and die in their devoir, like faithful and loyal Knights of St. John.

Scarcely was this done when out from their trenches came pouring the Moslem host, to sweep up the slope and over our poor defences. But so stubbornly did we fight that it was past the hour of nones when at length all resistance was beaten down and the victorious Moslem planted the banner of the Crescent on the ruins of St. Elmo. And the day on which St. Elmo fell was the twenty-third of June, the day of St. John the Baptist, patron saint of the Order of Knights Hospitallers of St. John!

For myself, when the assault began, I was stationed on the southern end of the ramparts, with young la Vallette, Polastra, de Guiral, and five other Knights. Opposing us were Dragut's Algerine corsairs, and it was to this fact that we owed our lives. No quarter was given elsewhere, but their piratical trade had taught these men that captives were a valuable form of merchandise, to be sold for a price in the bazaars of Tripoli or Algiers. A great body of them surrounded us when the castle was won, bidding us throw down our arms and yield, and promising to spare our lives if we obeyed. De

Guiral, being our senior, asked what we wished to do.

"For my part," he said, "I am in favor of accepting. We can do no good by dying, but if we live we may, by God's grace, still serve the true faith."

"But will they keep their word?" I asked. "Is it not merely a ruse to trick us into throwing down our swords, that they may slay us without danger?"

"Nay," he assured me, "they can be trusted. There is little enough good to be said of them, but we may grant them that credit; they are true to a promise."

"For myself," spoke up Polastra, "I would rather die than eke out a wretched life in slavery."

"And so say I!" agreed Wilhelm von Marck, a Knight of the German langue. "Herr Gott! Death rather than the oar and the lash."

"Let me point out," said de Guiral, "that we may escape or be ransomed from slavery, but there is no ransom from the grave. And no less a person than Jehan Parisot de la Vallette, who may be conceded to have done good service to Our Lord, in his youth pulled an oar for a year in the galley of Dragut the Algerine."

"My uncle?" asked young la Vallette, in astonishment. "The Grand Master?"

"Your uncle, the Grand Master," de Guiral affirmed. "Did you not know it?"

"No, by St. Ives! Strange that he should never have spoken thereof to me! Still," he reflected, "I have seen him but rarely until the siege began. However, that puts another face on the matter. What my uncle has done, I can do. I am for surrender."

In the end we agreed, and cast our swords on the ground. We were stripped, shackled, and marched down to the water-front, and that night lay down as slaves in the hold of an Algerine pirate ship. Exhausted by toil and wounds, it was long ere I slept, but at length I fell into an uneasy slumber, to dream of years of back-breaking labor at the oar, under a burning sun and beneath the overseer's cruel lash.

CHAPTER VII

Of Our Escape from the Algerine Corsairs; and the Journey Through the Catacombs

IF I seem, in these memoirs, to speak excessively of my own deeds, it is from no wish to exalt myself unduly above my fellows, but partly because this is, after all, my own story, and partly because I can best relate what I in person saw and did. For be assured that I was far from being alone in knightly acts; each one of the Order—nay, I might fairly say each one of all our forces—was so inspired by God and by the lofty example and high courage of la Vallette that to relate the full tale of heroic deeds then wrought would take a volume for each man and for no small number of the women as well. Truly, I do not think that so gallant a company of daring and devoted souls has ever, before or since, been gathered together in one place against one common foe! It is true that some of the younger Knights in St. Elmo appeared for a time to falter in their devoir, but this was not through cowardice; it was merely because they did not fully understand the Grand Master's policy, and having returned to their duty, they died as heroically as any. There was one man, I must admit, whose conduct was not altogether knightly, as I shall tell later, but I have no wish to condemn him; he has long since stood before the judgment seat of God.

The nine of us, then, were marched across the tongue of land on which St. Elmo stood, and were held under guard on the southern shore of Marza Muscetto. A fierce quarrel took place between our captors and a number of the Yeni-Tscheri who sought to slay us, and actual fighting was averted only by the officers. But in the end the Algerines made good their claim, and held us for ransom or for sale.

We were all wounded, though by good hap none gravely, and we were outworn from our long toil. Also, the heavy shackles on our legs galled us, and the tropic sun beat fiercely on our bare heads, so that we suffered in no light measure. De Guiral asked that we might have water, but none was brought, and we continued to thirst; I do not think, though, that this was deliberate cruelty—rather, indifference. At length, late in the afternoon, the Ottoman fleet sailed gaily up from its southern anchorage, and with music and streaming banners entered Marza Muscetto, the triumphant shouts and gun-fire of the galleys answering those from shore. We were hustled into a small boat and ferried out to an anchored galley, then driven down into the hold, where our shackles were undone, looped about a heavy iron bar which stood horizontal a span above the deck, and refastened, leaving us to stretch out as best we might on the rough planking. Food and water were brought, and we ate and drank eagerly, regretting only that there was not enough water to wash our wounds. Then after some talk of this and that we lay down to slumber; indeed, von Marck and one or two others composed themselves immediately after eating, and I remember envying them their peace of mind.

Our chief topic of conversation—indeed, it was little save cursing—was the things we had seen done between our surrender and our being brought over to Marza Muscetto. The Turkish commander, Mustapha Pasha, was a brutal man, and he caused the heads of de Miranda, the Bailiff of Negropont, and two others to be struck off and set on poles looking toward Il Borgo. It was shocking enough to see our dear companions thus treated with contempt, like the basest criminals, but a far worse spectacle was in store. A dozen or so bodies of Knights were brought down to the water's edge, stripped naked, lashed to planks, and scored on the bosoms with deep knife-cuts in the shape of the eight-pointed cross of St. John. Then they were set adrift on the Grand Harbor, the currents of air and water taking them over to St. Michael and St. Angelo. And to make the outrage complete, four of the Knights were still breathing when this was done! I am happy to say that when la Vallette learned of this infamy, and saw the disfigured bodies of his companions, he at once ordered the heads of a hundred or more Turkish prisoners to be struck off and shot from our cannon into the infidel lines, by way of teaching the Paynim a lesson in humanity.

I might add here that we Christians lost, during the siege of St. Elmo, about fifteen hundred souls, among them being a hundred and twenty-three Knights of the Order. Of the infidels, eight thousand perished, their greatest loss—as we learned from our captors—being Dragut, who died shortly after the castle was taken. It may well be guessed that neither de Guiral nor I revealed to our guards the identity of the man whose shot struck down the famous Algerine.

On the day following our surrender, food and drink were again brought to us, together with a few cloths and a tub of water, that we might wash ourselves and cleanse our wounds. I do not know whether or not our jailers intended cruelty in this last, for it was sea water, and smarted mightily, but if so they defeated their own aim, it being well known that salt water is far more healing than fresh. Having eaten, drunk, slept, and washed, we felt much better, and began to discuss our situation. Shackled next to me was the Chevalier Fortuny, the ingenious deviser of the fire-hoop, and I saw him plucking at a nail which protruded an inch or so from the planking.

"The accursed thing jabbed into me as I slept," he answered my look of inquiry, and went on working, tugging and wrenching at it, but with no success.

"Let me try," suggested von Marck, on my other side, and leaning across me he gripped the nail with his fingers and thumb, pulled vigorously, and out it came. Fortuny stared in amazement.

"Por Dios!" he exclaimed. "But you are strong."

Von Marck chuckled with gratification.

"Is it not so?" he agreed. He was vain as a child of his enormous strength, though humble enough in other matters—a good man through and through, and far from stupid, as is so often the case, God seeming to average His favors, and to conjoin strong muscles with a weak head. "I can lay a silver thaler across my fore and middle fingers, so—" he illustrated with a gesture "—and placing my thumb on it, bend it double."

Fortuny nodded.

"Thanks," he said, briefly, and fell to gazing

thoughtfully at the nail, which von Marck had handed him.

Presently he took to examining the padlock of his shackles, looking from that to the nail and back again, until at length he asked von Marck:

"Brother, would you bend this for me?"

"Of a surety," replied the German, proud to display his strength. Fortuny indicated that he wanted the iron bent at right angles, some two inches from the end, and von Marck gave a wrench, then handed the nail back, saying:

"There!"

Fortuny took it, busied himself for a few moments with the padlocks, then removed the shackles from his legs.

"Herr Gott!" exploded von Marck. "Can you do as much for us all? And where did you learn that?"

"It is but a sleight," answered the Castilian. "I can, I think, free us all, yes."

Word was passed along the line of what Fortuny had done, and de Guiral at once took charge, commanding that we wait until night ere proceeding further; also, he ordered Fortuny to replace his gyves, lest one of the corsairs, coming down into the hold, give the alarm.

The hold where we were confined ran nearly the entire length of the vessel, being eighty or ninety feet in length by twenty in width, and we had it to ourselves save for a pile of stolen merchandise at the far end; we were the only prisoners. The sole communication with the deck above was by a hatchway and a short flight of steps near the bow, and this opening admitted the only light we had; now, in the morning, the sun poured down there, its reflected rays illuminating more or less the whole space, but in the afternoon we would sit in twilight, while at night the blackness was Stygian.

"So far as I can tell from the sounds," de Guiral whispered to us, who gathered as close as we could, "there are but three of the infidels on board; the others are busied about the siege works, leaving only these to guard us. As soon as it is dark, Fortuny will release us—you can do it by sense of touch?" he inquired of the Castilian, who replied:

"Surely."

"Excellent!" said de Guiral. "You will release von Marck first, and he will take his place at the foot of the stairs, ready to deal with any interruption. When all are free, I will try to entice one of the guards down, and von Marck, stationed behind the ladder, will care for him. A second will come to see what detains the first, and him also will we manage. But the third will be suspicious and will not descend, so you, Polastra, will take the weapons from one of the guards as soon as the second is dead, and going on deck you will despatch the third as quietly as possible. Do not let him give the alarm if it can by any means be avoided. We will follow on deck and make a dash for liberty, either by swimming or in a small boat if one is at hand—somehow, at least. Is all fully understood?"

"Chevalier," I offered, "may I not have the honor of dealing with the third man? Not that I question for an instant our brother's skill or hardihood, but we are almost certain to find a dagger on one or the other of the first two, and a native has taught me the art of casting a knife. If I can bring down the third guard from a distance, your plan is that much more likely to succeed."

Polastra was very reluctant to yield his place to me, and an argument followed, but in the end it was decided that the task should be mine, and with that we all lay down again to wait the appointed time.

As the sun rose higher, the heat grew stifling in the 'tween-decks, and the air was so dead and motionless that, naked though we were, we panted miserably for breath. But the long afternoon wore finally to a close, and about dusk one of our jailers came down to inspect us. We all pretended apathy save de Guiral, who lay on his back, his eyes closed, his mouth hanging wide, his bosom heaving as a rattling breath drew in and out through his throat.

The Algerine carried a torch, and by its light he looked us over one by one, making sure our shackles were fast. Then he departed, first bestowing on each of us a hearty kick, which he administered as solemnly as though it were part of his daily prayers. Fortuny then set to work, and in a few minutes we were free, von Marck taking his assigned post, while the rest of us lay still. I cannot say how the others felt, but for my part I was tense and eager, trembling from head to foot with excitement, even as I have seen dogs do ere they are turned loose on a bear. This nervousness before action has always afflicted me, but happily it disappears when once the fight begins.

Presently de Guiral set up a most distressful moaning, joined with agonized cries for water. At length the oblong of the hatchway was blotted out by the head and shoulders of the guard, who growled a remark in his own tongue. Young la Vallette answered him, and the man grunted some reply, then disappeared for a time, and shortly came climbing down, a torch in one hand and in the other a leathern bucket. As his feet touched the deck, von Marck slipped around the ladder, silent as a bodiless spirit, and struck the man with his clenched fist at the base of the brain. The victim of that terrible blow slumped to the deck, and before I reached him he was dead.

I searched him for weapons, finding a scimitar—a beautiful Damascus blade, it was—and a thin dagger of the sort known to the French as a miséricorde, evidently stolen in some raid on France. It was a long, narrow blade, intended to find the joints of a wounded foeman's armor, to administer the coup de grâce, and therefore neither heavy enough nor balanced right to be ideal for throwing; the hilt overweighted the blade. Still, it could be made to serve. The scimitar I handed to de Guiral, who hid it under his body.

We returned to our positions, von Marck extinguishing the torch, and by and by another head and shoulders appeared in the hatchway.

"Ali!" called the newcomer, and after waiting a moment: "Ali!"

Receiving no answer, he grunted, went for a torch, and came scrambling down, to be dealt with as the first had been. Then I took my place at the foot of the ladder, the miséricorde held by the point, while I waited for the appearance of the third man. I had not long to wait, for in a few minutes his dark silhouette blotted out a space of sky and stars as he listened. Before he could speak, I snapped my arm forward, and the dagger, guided by the holy St. John, caught the unbeliever square in the center of the throat, driving through to pierce his spine. If I say it myself, it was a pretty cast, considering the darkness, and the man was dead ere he knew what had befallen him.

Bounding up the ladder, I plucked out the dagger and rolled the body aside, out of the way of my companions, who instantly followed me. De Guiral was right; there were no more infidels on board, and we had the galley to ourselves. For a moment I had a wild idea of taking possession of it and sailing it back to the Bay of Galleys, between St. Angelo and la Sangle, but brief thought showed me that this would be impossible; we lay midway of Marza Muscetto, and must run the gauntlet of the whole Turkish fleet, which could not fail to see that there was something wrong. There was no gunfire in progress, but lights twinkled amid the ruins of St. Elmo and on Point Dragut, wherefore we knew the Turks were active about something; indeed, shouts and cries came to us across the quiet water.

I made my way to the stern, where I found a small boat trailing at the end of a rope, and the others, following, lowered themselves one by one into it, von Marck picking up the oars which by good hap lay in the bottom. I cut the rope, and we set out for the nearest shore, not more than a hundred paces distant, the tongue of land west of Mount Sceberras.

It was fortunate that the water was still, for the skiff was dangerously overloaded, but in a few minutes we landed, de Guiral leading us back from the shore to where we found a hiding-place among the rocks and bushes.

"By Our Lady of Philermo!" said Fortuny. "I am glad to be here! An inch of freeboard, with the water lapping the gunwales, is no encouragement to one who cannot swim! What now, de Guiral?"

"Has anyone aught to suggest?" asked our leader, and I offered:

"Why not cross this piece of land and swim for St. Angelo? It is not more than three-quarters of a mile, and seems our best chance of eluding the besiegers."

"But you have just heard Fortuny say that he cannot swim," spoke up Polastra. "Furthermore, three-quarters of a mile is vastly beyond my powers; I might make fifty paces, but no more."

"We can doubtless find some planks to support you two, and we others can push you."

"By your leave, Sir Richard," responded Fortuny. "It is not for me. A wise woman has predicted a watery death in my horoscope, and I would prefer to avoid the sea. But that need not hinder. Go, you, and Polastra and I will make our way around by land."

"The lines are drawn around St. Michael and Il Borgo," said von Marck. "You will but fall into the hands of the Paynim."

"That is a chance we will take."

"Nay," said de Guiral, "all or none. Sir Richard, your plan is discarded. Has anyone another?"

"Here is an alternative," I suggested. "In all likelihood, we can make our way along the shore as far as Ras Hanzier; it is not likely that the infidels will be there. And once at Ras Hanzier, I can guide you through the catacombs to Città Notable, where we can get food and clothing, and learn how best we may elude the Paynim and make our way through the lines to St. Angelo."

"If through the catacombs," asked von Marck, "why not direct to Il Borgo? Do they not lead into the crypt of St. Lawrence?"

"They did," I told him. "But de la Mara and I intercepted a band of infidels near the crypt and slew them, whereupon the Grand Master had that passage walled off."

"So-o?" said the German. "Herr Gott, that was well done, Sir Richard. I had not heard of it. Well, ho for Città Notable."

Stumbling, falling, bruised by rocks and raked by bushes, we made our way along the shore for something over a mile—nearly two, indeed. It was no pleasant journey, for the night air was nipping and eager, the stones were hard, and we were stark naked and barefoot. But in the end we made it, and after some search I found the opening of the catacombs, hidden amid rocks and brush. Fortuny had brought the torches of our guards, together with flint and steel taken from the bodies, and when we reached a safe depth within the rocky tunnel de Guiral called a halt, bidding the Castilian give us light.

"No need, now, of stumbling along and hurting ourselves in the darkness," he said. "Besides, Sir Richard will be better able to guide us if he can see."

This was true enough, and accepting the torch Fortuny handed me, I set off at a good round pace for Città Notable, the others following close at my heels.

It was far from an easy trip, that one through the bowels of the earth. Measured in a straight line, Ras Hanzier is between five and six miles from Città Notable, but so many were the twists and turns of our path that we traveled at least twice that distance. Then, too, we lost ourselves four several times, and had to retrace our steps and hunt for the true path, so that long before we came out into the blessed light of day I almost regretted the expedition Juan and I had led against the invaders —and I certainly regretted la Vallette's decision to wall off the crypt; but for that, our journey had been short and simple.

During the march, we well-nigh lost our commander. At a certain place the path narrowed for twenty yards or so to a shelf less than an ell in width, skirting the edge of a bottomless gulf. As we were proceeding in single file along this ledge, I heard a cry behind me, and turned to see de Guiral, his arms flung wide, pitch sideways over the black depths; a loose stone, rolling under his foot, had thrown him. For an instant my heart stood still, but von Marck, directly behind the Chevalier, shot out a lightning-quick arm and caught de Guiral's wrist. De Guiral swung free, his feet over the terrible drop, and I thanked God for von Marck's mighty strength, for bracing himself on the path he lifted that full-grown man back to safety as easily as Marjorie Chauntrey would have lifted her Bartholomew baby. De Guiral leaned against the wall and rubbed his shoulder, which had been nigh unjointed.

"My thanks," he said to the German. "I hope some day to return the favor."

Von Marck waved a huge brown paw in acknowledgment.

"It is nothing," he rejoined. "Let us be on our way."

We were foot-sore and weary ere we reached the end of our underground journey, but shortly after dawn we came out into the sunlight within the purlieus of Città Notable, and at the mouth of the catacombs an argument rose as to which of us should go for help; none cared to present himself naked in the streets of the town. At length de Guiral appointed me, saying:

"I would go myself, but I am sore lame." And in truth he had made the latter part of the journey only with assistance, for he was weak from his wounds, and had turned his ankle badly when the stone rolled under his foot.

I liked the task not at all, but he was my senior, and I obeyed. The first person I met was a young woman on her way to the fountain for water, and when she caught sight of me she shrieked, dropped her jar, which crashed to bits on the stone pavement, and she incontinently fled, screaming at the top of her lungs. Not until then had I realized what a fearsome spectacle I must present, bearded, naked, smeared with blood, scratched and torn by briars, and with a naked poniard in my hand. Had she raised the townsmen, it is not improbable that they would have slaughtered me before I could explain, but by good fortune the first to answer her cries was a priest, who, being a man of God, was not easily stampeded by terror. He heard me out, smiled, and said:

"Get you back into hiding, my son. I will bring aid."

He was as good as his word, for within half an

hour he led to us a group of men with clothing, food, and wine, and after ministering to us they escorted us to various houses within the town, where a leech tended our wounds and we were all cared for and allowed to rest and sleep.

About dusk de Guiral sent for me.

"Sir Richard," he said, "I must perforce remain here for a few days; the chirurgeon says I must have rest. And in sooth this foot will not bear my weight." I could see that the limb was swollen to twice its natural size. "So," he continued, "I appoint you in my stead to lead our party to St. Angelo, and to report to the Grand Master. I am told that the Moslems have invested Il Borgo, but have not yet drawn their lines about St. Michael. Guides will therefore take you to the latter place, whence boats will set you across the Bay of Galleys to the castle."

"Under favor, sir," I replied, "guides are not needed. I know the road well."

"It will do no harm," he answered, dryly, "to have some forty or fifty brave and well armed Maltese with you, in case of wandering parties from the infidel camp."

I saw the justice of this, acceded, received further instructions, and as soon as night had fully come we set out, the escort going on foot, though horses were provided for us of the Order.

By good hap, none interfered with us, and we came safe to St. Michael, where the commander, Don Antonio de Zanoguerra, received us with all honor. Our escort, thirty-five in number, had been so fired by the tale of St. Elmo and of our escape from the corsairs that they wished to volunteer, and it was at the head of a goodly party that I marched at length into St. Angelo.

The Grand Master had been warned of our coming, and welcomed us in the Council Hall, as many of the Knights as were off duty attending to hear our story. La Vallette embraced us warmly, and I told what had befallen us since the taking of St. Elmo, for he had already had word of the storming of the castle; three or four of the Maltese volunteers, escaping the general destruction, had swum the Grand Harbor, to carry the word. I am happy to say that Hamilcar Xuereb and the man who brought me Lady Madeleine's rose were of this number.

Amid an eager and attentive silence I told of our adventures, giving all praise to de Guiral, von Marck, and Fortuny, who had made possible our escape; and when I had finished, the Knights broke out in many expressions of delight and astonishment, crowding in to grasp our hands.

"You have borne yourselves like true paladins, my children," said la Vallette. "I mourn the

Brethren who were lost in St. Elmo, but after all they fell like true chevaliers, in all duty and honor, nor do I doubt that they have already gone to their just reward. Nor do I question that with such brave and gallant men we shall make head against the infidel, though their number be as the sands of the sea."

So he dismissed us, and we went to our quarters.

On the way I was halted by Don Diego de Espinosa, who stopped to congratulate me warmly.

"I am but now from duty, Sir Richard," he said, "and hurried back in the hope of hearing your tale from your own lips, some word thereof having reached me through the soldiers. I gather that you have won much well deserved glory. My felicitations! Though," he added, with a slight smile, "in view of the purpose which brings us here, I cannot avoid some small feeling of envy."

Much as I disliked the man, and insincere though I felt him to be, there was no denying that he was mannerly and well bred, and I replied with courtesy equal to his own, thanking him for his words.

"Nor do I doubt," I assured him, "that you will find as great or greater opportunity for honorable advancement, and will do full justice to it when it comes."

He thanked me in turn, and we parted, our mouths full of honeyed words, our hearts of dislike

—though just how bitter the dislike was, I did not know until later.

I was preparing for bed, when my door was thrown open and de la Mara burst in.

"Ricardo mio!" he cried, flinging his arms about my neck and kissing me on both cheeks. "Por Dios, it is yourself! We have mourned you for lost, and the good God restores you to us. Ah, amigo de mi corazón!" And he hugged me again, I returning his embraces with scarcely less fervor, for I loved him dearly, and had not thought to see him again.

"But dress and come with me," he said, presently. "Certain other of your friends crave to greet you."

"Juan," I told him, "I am weary past all belief. Will it not keep till the morrow?"

"No, no, no!" he vowed. "English fish! Ice-blooded man of the north! It will not keep. It is the Lady Madeleine and the Countess Carmela who bade me bring you to them. Come, fish-man, stir yourself!"

After all, it would be good to see these ladies, so I replaced the boots and doublet which I had thrown off and followed Juan to the Zerafa Palace. The countess was the first to greet me, using the fashion Juan had done, her arms about my neck, her lips against my cheek.

"So!" she said. "It is our paladin come back from the jaws of death. I give you greeting, Sir

Richard. Have you slain many of the Paynim? A goodly number?"

"Some few," I told her, smiling. "Among others, Dragut."

"What?" exploded Juan. "In good sooth, Ricardo? Tell us of it!"

"A chance shot," I replied. "No great merit of mine. The tale will keep." And I turned to the Lady Madeleine.

Her greeting was more restrained than the Countess de Zerafa's, though equally sincere, for as she laid her hand in mine I saw tears in her eyes, and at first she could not speak. But at length she managed a few words.

"I . . . I greet you, Sir Richard. It is—how do you say?—it is much joy to us all to see you once more. . . ." Her mouth quivered, and she could not go on, the tears overflowing her lids and rolling down her cheeks. She wiped them with her kerchief, then smiled and said: "I am silly, like a child. You will forgive? But it is good to see you."

I assured her that forgiveness was easy, and for a time we talked of the siege, then Juan made my excuses.

"Ricardo is weary," he told the ladies. "And he craves his bed. You will pardon us?"

And on my promise to come at the first opportunity and tell them all my adventures they let us go.

One more interruption stood between me and my rest, for as we crossed the outer bailey of St. Angelo we were waylaid by Evans and Xuereb, come to congratulate me on my escape. I was glad to see them, especially the latter, for until reassured by the Grand Master, I had feared that he was lost in the storming. But when I said as much, he replied:

"It will take more than these infidels to slay me. But how of yourself, Sir Richard? Were you much hurt in the mêlée?"

"A few trifling wounds. Of no particular account. It was our good Hamilcar," I told Juan, "who saved my life at the taking of the castle." And I recounted how he had slain Yussef, while Xuereb looked down and shuffled his feet in embarrassment, protesting that it was nothing.

"It was much, much!" Juan declared. "Come to me to-morrow, and that shot shall be paid for with a handful of gold."

"How of you, David?" I inquired. "Are you married yet? I seem to recall that you were betrothed to a maid in Il Borgo."

He grinned sheepishly and nodded.

"Brother William, chaplain of St. Angelo, performed the ceremony a sennight back. But she was not a maid, Sir Richard; a widow. A widow is ever better than a maid, having had more experience in devising a man's comfort. And my Fiametta is an excellent cook. You should taste her olla. And her roast goose is fit for the Grand Master's own table."

I laughed and slapped him on the back.

"May you be happy with her," I said. "I shall hope to meet her ere long. Perchance to taste her cooking."

He glowed with pleasure at this, and saying good-night to him and Xuereb, Juan and I went our way.

As we walked, Juan thought it best to admonish me.

"Is it well, Ricardo," he asked, "to be so familiar with the lower classes? You know our Order is of high-born men, so much so that the commonalty must step aside from the pavement on meeting a Knight. Yet you chat with these men of low birth in most friendly manner. Is it wise, think you?"

I chuckled.

"It has been my lot, in youth," I told him, "to be thrown much with men of that sort, and I think I know how to meet them. Have you ever seen any of them show me discourtesy, or use undue familiarity toward me?"

"Por Dios, no! Nor would I care to be the one who did!"

"Then spare your fears, my friend. Beyond which, I have often found as much courage and kindliness among such men as among those of noble birth."

"That is true," he admitted, heartily. "They fight as well as we do, and die as bravely."

"Their ways are not our ways," I went on, "nor would I choose my associates—my intimates, rather —from their ranks. But except for the chance of birth they are much the same as ourselves."

He shook his head doubtfully.

"Noble blood is different from common blood," he said. "At least, so I have been taught. Well, according to reason, each thing in its season. Do you go your way, and I will go mine. Though," he added, with some wistfulness, "would that I could command their loyalty and affection as you seem to do. Oh, my men are good soldiers, and obey orders promptly, but I question if any of them would give his life for mine, or deeply mourn my loss. And I am convinced that any who has followed you would lose an arm rather than his leader." He changed the subject. "At all events, here we are at our quarters, and we can mark this day with white, Ricardo mio—the day on which you have come back to us."

That night, as I lay down to sleep, the Turkish guns took up anew their now familiar thunder, this time pouring their shot and shell against the walls of St. Angelo.

CHAPTER VIII

Of the Fight in the Water; and of Our Amazons

IMMEDIATELY on the fall of St. Elmo, Mustapha began the investment of St. Angelo and St. Michael, devoting the most of his attention to the former. By his orders, the outlying houses in Il Borgo—such as had escaped our demolition—were razed or burned, and trenches were thrown up, the Turkish artillery being so placed as to batter the castle walls, while from across the Grand Harbor the basilicas, mounted among the ruins of St. Elmo, hurled their giant missiles against the fortifications on that side. A number of heavy guns, too, were dragged up the slopes of Mount Sceberras and planted near the summit, where their elevation gave them a notable advantage.

Under la Vallette's instruction, we built barricades of stone in the streets of Il Borgo, making them as strong as possible, and garrisoning these impromptu fortifications. It was the Grand Master's idea to defend the place step by step, retreating only when we must, and not taking refuge in the citadel of St. Angelo until forced to do so; the

194

vital thing, he said, was to hold out until aid came from Sicily.

Also, the Turks opened trenches at the foot of Mount Corradino, whence shot and shell rained on St. Michael and la Sangle, and they launched a sudden attack, in the nature of a surprise, on Il Borgo. This well-nigh succeeded, the sentry not giving the alarm until the Moslems were fairly up to our walls. However, we repulsed them, and the sentry was brought before la Vallette, to whom he pleaded in excuse that he was suffering from moon-blindness and did not see the attack gathering. The Grand Master sent for Messer Gaddi.

"This man avers," he told the chirurgeon, "that he was stricken with moon-blindness, which was his reason for not giving the alarm. Will you examine him and determine whether or not he speaks the truth?"

Messer Gaddi uttered a contemptuous snort.

"Moon-blindness!" he said. "An old wives' tale —sheer superstition! But I will test his eyesight and report."

The man was examined, his vision was found to be excellent, and Messer Gaddi reported to the Grand Master that his failure was due either to slumber or to treachery. And with that la Vallette had the sentry publicly hanged, both to punish him and to encourage the others.

Mustapha made several attempts to bring his galleys around into the Grand Harbor, that he might take St. Angelo in the rear, but so heavy a fire was poured on the ships that this could not be done. De la Mara was in charge at the Bastion of Castile, de Guiral had been placed in command of the artillery of St. Angelo, and Frederick de Toledo, son of the Viceroy of Sicily, had under his care the guns of the Bastion of the Spur, at the tip of the promontory of la Sangle. This last Knight did not share his father's vacillation of character, but was a most daring and determined youth, and joined with the others in sweeping the Grand Harbor with so fierce and concentrated a gun-fire that Mustapha must needs give over his attempts to run the passage. And in consequence of this, we were treated to a marvellous and vastly interesting spectacle.

One day a week or so after the siege of St. Angelo began, Sir Oliver Starkey and I were on the ramparts overlooking the Grand Harbor. He had his optic glass—which went everywhere with him—and was watching some galleys that were coming up from the east.

"Reinforcements," he said. "By the banners, it should be none other than Hassem."

"Who is he?" I asked, and Sir Oliver smiled.

"No mean antagonist," he rejoined, "for all his

youthful arrogance and conceit. He is son to the famous Barbarossa, the Red-Beard, and is allied by marriage to Dragut, having taken one of the latter's daughters for his first wife. It was Hassem who commanded at the notable sieges of Mazarquivir and of Oran. Oh, we shall have some good fighting, doubt it not! However, by God's grace, we too have reinforcements, though fewer, no doubt, than Hassem brings."

"How so?"

"Have you not heard? La Vallette has brought in five companies from Città Notable, where they were not needed—"

"I knew that, yes."

"And four galleys, sent by Don Garcia de Toledo, brought us forty Knights and seven hundred Spanish arquebusiers and men-at-arms."

I thought this over, finally saying:

"That seems but scant aid for Sicily to send."

"Oh, it is merely an hors-d'oeuvre; the main dish will come later." Here Sir Oliver broke off to laugh. "The manner of their coming was delicious!" he said. "They were under command of Don Juan de Cordova, who had strict orders from the viceroy not to land if St. Elmo had fallen. But he anchored off Pietra Negra, on the western coast, and sent one of the Brethren ashore for news. This Knight, not sharing the viceroy's timidity, learned of the storming but kept it secret, and the whole detachment was landed, under command of the Chevalier de Robles, one of our most illustrious members. De Robles, being as crafty as he is brave, led his men to the eastern shore of the English Port without being discovered by the Turks. He sent a swimmer to the Grand Master, and to-night, after compline, a flotilla of boats will bring the soldiers to St. Angelo."

And I too laughed, remarking:

"It will be a sore blow to Don Garcia, when he learns of it."

"H'mph!" snorted Sir Oliver. "Let him stew in his own juice!"

Some activity on the western slopes of Mount Sceberras caught my eye, and I pointed it out to Sir Oliver, asking:

"What is going forward there?"

He turned the optic glass in that direction, watched for a moment, and burst out:

"Pardi! As I live and breathe, they are dragging a galley across the mountain! Look else." And he handed me the glass.

It was even as he said. A path had been smoothed over the rocks, and aided by ropes and great rollers, hundreds of slaves were hauling one of the Turkish galleys over the tongue of land and easing it down the rugged slopes to the harbor.

Mustapha was wise enough to have this toilsome work done by Christians, so we could not fire upon them, and during the next five days there was naught for it but to crowd the ramparts and watch, cursing and passing the optic glass from hand to hand, while ship after ship slid down the mountain and took the water with a smash of leaping spray. And in the end, no fewer than eighty galleys, some of them the very largest, were afloat on the surface of the Grand Harbor.

When this labor was completed, Mustapha sent a messenger to la Vallette, bearing a proposal for our surrender. The letter promised that if we would yield the island we should receive honorable terms and a free passage for the Knights, their followers, and all their effects, to Sicily. The messenger was a Christian slave, and the letter, which he read aloud, was in French, so that we all, standing about the Council Hall, understood it, and many an anxious eye was bent on la Vallette to see how he was taking it.

But the Grand Master sat utterly impassive till the reading was finished, when he inquired:

"Have you done?"

"Yes, most noble sir," the slave replied. "That is all."

La Vallette waved his hand.

"Take him out and hang him," was all his answer.

In terror, the envoy prostrated himself at the Grand Master's feet.

"No, no!" he begged. "Have mercy, most gracious sir! I am but a poor slave, forced against my will to obey my master's commands. It were not just to punish me for his acts. Have pity, have mercy!"

La Vallette considered for a time, then relented.

"So be it," he said. "Your life is spared. But tell Mustapha that should he again insult me with such a message, not only will I refuse to entertain it, but I will have his envoy crammed living into my largest gun and shot back whence he came."

The slave rose, babbling thanks, and la Vallette gave orders to conduct him over the works, that he might report to Mustapha how strongly we were defended. This was done, and from the landward rampart Espinosa, who, with myself, had the man in charge, called attention to the wide fosse about our fortress.

"There," he said, pointing to the ditch, "is what portion of Malta we will yield to your master. But it is deep enough to bury him and all his followers!"

As the envoy was being led out of the great gate, I stopped him.

"You are a Christian," I reminded him, "and you owe no allegiance to Mustapha. Will you not remain and join your fortunes to ours, to the glory of God and the salvation of your soul?"

He hesitated, and seemed to debate the question, but at length shook his head.

"Why not?" I urged. "You have not said the Fatihah?"

"Nay," he answered, "I am a good Christian. But you cannot hold out; Malta must in the end be taken, and then my captivity would be far worse than before—chains, the dungeon, the bastinado, perchance death. Nay, tempt me not!"

And breaking from me, he departed, almost running.

After all, I could not greatly blame him, for he was an old man, in whom the flame of life burned low, and having been for many years a slave, he had lost the fiery spirit which animates a youth and a free man. As we turned away, Don Diego smiled a tight-lipped smile and said:

"I do not think that Mustapha will send us any further envoys with proposals for surrender."

I answered his smile with another, saying:

"For their sake, I hope that he does not; the fate promised by the Grand Master would not be enviable."

Don Diego shrugged.

"For myself, I could wish to see it," he rejoined.

"It would be an interesting experiment, shooting a live man from a cannon."

I felt a shiver of disgust, but said nothing; wanton cruelty has ever been repugnant to me, but there was naught to be gained by provoking a quarrel. Of course it must not be supposed that I was in any way criticizing the Grand Master; his position justified his threat, and my distaste was for Espinoza, who could find pleasure in the spectacle.

About this time a man presented himself, one midnight, before our outer lines, craving admittance. He was led before the Grand Master, where he gave his name as Lascaris, saying that he was a Greek, taken captive in youth by the Turks. Accepting Islam, he had risen to high command in the Ottoman army—his dress and manner bore him out in this—but since the beginning of the siege his conscience had given him no rest, and he begged to join his Christian brethren once more.

La Vallette at first suspected treachery, but the man spoke in so convincing and sincere a manner that in the end the Grand Master believed, and accepted him as a recruit, merely warning him:

"You know what will be your end if you are retaken."

"I shall not be retaken," Lascaris assured him. "Better to die under the Cross than live under the Crescent. And I am sick to death of these base idolaters, with their mosques, their eternal 'la ilaha illa-llahu,' * their ninety-nine Beautiful Names, their greasy, pinguid, garlic-reeking concubines. Also, I yearn beyond all words for the rock-girt isles and blue hills of Greece, and for the wine of Cyprus, which is forbidden to Islam."

La Vallette commanded that the deserter be given, at once, a goblet of Cyprian wine, and it was amusing to see Lascaris' gratitude; as the ruddy liquid flowed down his throat he lifted his eyes to Heaven, like a barnyard fowl drinking, and he set down the empty goblet with a long sigh and a smile more eloquent than words. I would not have believed that a man could so desire some special article of food or drink; doubtless the fact of its being forbidden made it doubly precious in his thoughts.

Lascaris served with distinction through the remainder of the siege, and his first act was to make it known to the Grand Master that the Turks were planning a raid on our vessels, impounded in the Bay of Galleys, between Il Borgo and la Sangle.

"Also, and more particularly," said the Greek, "he is preparing to send his galleys into the bay between la Sangle and Mount Corradino. This, that he may secure a concentration of artillery against St. Michael."

La Vallette thanked Lascaris for this informa-

* "There is no God but Allah."

tion, and acted on it forthwith. The Bay of Galleys was already protected by a heavy iron chain, effectually precluding a naval attack at that point, and a number of workmen were now given the task of setting a row of piles from the point of la Sangle to the base of Mount Corradino, thus closing off the westernmost of the bays. It was necessary to perform the task at night, under cover of darkness, but even so the Turkish artillery harassed the men, and our guns replied. Half a score or so of the workers were lost, and two of the barges from which they toiled were sunk, but in about a week the piles were driven and fastened together with heavy chains wrapped again and again about their tops. An effective barrier was thus provided against the Turkish fleet.

This barrier was the direct cause of one of the most desperate and savage encounters of the whole siege, an encounter which brought me no small measure of renown, though my share was far from being undertaken in the hope of glory; it was merely that an opportunity presented itself to serve Christ and the Order, and I tried to do my duty.

Two days after the palisade was finished, la Vallette sent me with a message to Don Antonio de Zanoguerra, commanding at St. Michael. By crossing from the water-front of St. Angelo to a point

midway of the promontory of la Sangle, the passage
was easy enough, the only danger being from some
chance arquebusier in the lines before Il Borgo. But
since for the greater part of the journey I could be
sheltered by the hulls of our galleys, the risk was
practically naught, and shortly after vespers I had
Xuereb set me across in a light skiff. As we went,
great dark clouds were banking up above the hori-
zon, promising rain, and the air was filled with a
peculiar yellow light; the clouds themselves, reflect-
ing the low sun, glowed orange and red and purple
over a restless sea which took on strange, unnatural
colors from the sky. A slight breeze was making,
too, and all things presaged one of the fierce thun-
derstorms which at times sweep the Mediterranean.
Xuereb nodded toward the clouds as he swayed on
the oars.

"We shall have weather, Sir Richard," he commented, and I answered:

"So I see. I hope we may discharge our errand
and return ere the storm breaks."

He grinned at me.

"For one so indifferent to a shower of steel and
lead, you are oddly concerned for a shower of
water."

I shrugged, replying:

"I do not so much mind death in battle—that is
in the line of our devoir—but I should vastly dis-

like to die of a phthisis or a pleurisy. A little more weight on those oars, good Xuereb!"

Reaching St. Michael, I delivered the Grand Master's letter to Don Antonio, and while he dictated the reply to his secretary I amused myself with gazing from the window toward the Grand Harbor. It was fully dark by now, and the flashes of the Turkish guns were plainly seen against the blackness of the night; great tongues of orange flame leaped and disappeared, but so steady was the gun-fire as a whole that the entire sky glowed continually, lighted by the weird flames, while vast billows of smoke rolled seaward on the breeze. And now flares of white light danced and flickered in the distance, and from afar came a low rumbling, an undertone to the thunder of the guns. Looking toward the new-built palisade, I thought to mark some activity there, and wondered what it could be; the work, I had understood, was finished. While I strained my eyes, trying to make out what was on foot, a young Knight came bursting into the room.

"Your Excellency!" he cried. "The Turks are attacking our palisade!"

Don Antonio sprang to his feet.

"What?" he demanded. "What?"

The Knight repeated his statement, amplifying it.

"The sentry at the Spur reports that a body of

Turks have swum in with axes from the galleys, and are hewing at the piles. There are fifty or more, he says."

"Por Dios!" exclaimed Don Antonio. "What is to do? Let me think! We have no boats nearer than the Bay of Galleys, and ere we could bring them around to this side of la Sangle——"

"Your Excellency," I broke in, "may I offer a suggestion? Let me have a hundred men, good swimmers, and I will lead them against the Turks by water. It is the quickest way."

He stared at me for a moment, with narrowed eyes, then:

"Sangre de Cristo, Sir Richard, what daring! Still, you are right. Pedro——" to the young Knight "——ring the alarm bell, parade the men, and let Sir Richard select his party. Make haste."

The young Knight—Pedro Alvares he was, of the Castilian langue—obeyed, and as I emerged into the courtyard of St. Michael I found the garrison assembling by the light of torches. When all were in line I spoke to them.

"Men," I cried, "I want a hundred volunteers for a most desperate venture—for death or glory. They must be strong swimmers, all."

Only about sixty strode forward, though it was no lack of courage held the others back, but inexpertness in the water. Having got my men, I dismissed the others, but they hung around, buzzing excitedly, to see what was on foot.

"A body of Turkish axemen are destroying our palisade," I told my troop. "We are to fight them off. Strip, keeping only your shoes and your knives." And I set them the example by throwing off my own clothes.

In no long time they stood naked before me, to the tune of many a rough jest from their comrades.

"Your first bath since last you were caught in the rain, Hannibal!"

"At last, Sancho, you will rid yourself of your lice—give thanks to Sir Richard!"

"Matteo, should you die in the venture, you will at least go clean to Heaven."

"Nay, the holy angels will clothe him ere letting him enter the gate of Paradise—consider how shocked the Holy Mother would be to see our hairy Matteo in that guise! She would think him some ape from Ind!"

This last verged perilously close on blasphemy, and I rebuked the speaker sharply, bidding him be silent.

When all were ready, I took a Maltese knife from one of those who remained behind, and led my volunteers out toward the Spur, amid shouts and encouragements.

THE FIGHT IN THE WATER.

"A brisk walk, men," I told them. "We must be in time, but dare not arrive winded."

Anxious to join battle as quickly as possible, I marched my troop for about a quarter of a mile along the shore toward the Spur, then bade them remove their shoes and take to the water.

"Knives in your teeth," I said. "Follow me!"

Splash after splash, like seals diving from the rocks, we went in, striking out toward the palisade, some two hundred paces distant. I set an easy stroke, that none might be tired, and we kept well together, soon drawing near enough to hear plainly the thudding of axes, the oaths and cries of the workmen. In the murky light of the guns we drew close before the Turks knew that danger was near, then one of them, glancing up, discovered us.

"Allah!" he shouted. "Giaour! Giaour! The heathen, the heathen!"

"For God and St. John!" I called. "Charge!" And I flung myself into a racing stroke.

All about us the water boiled with threshing arms and legs, and before the Turks could gather themselves we were among them.

Then began as fierce and deadly a fight as ever was fought on sea or land. The Turks were brave, and defended themselves right valiantly, but an axe is an unwieldy thing in the water, and for hand-to-hand work the long Maltese knife is the deadliest weapon ever yet devised by man. Body to body, we struck and gripped and stabbed, guided only by that strange half light that filled the heavens. Oaths and screams went up, grunts and curses and groans, choked into bubbling gurgles as the salt water gushed into open mouths. Above water and below we fought, twining about like snakes, wrenching and twisting, using knife and knee and fist and tooth. Faces came and went, faces bare or bearded, axes rose and fell, knives gleamed and stabbed, dark eyes glared at us, white teeth shone, and naked bodies floated about or brushed against us as momentarily we sank and rose once more. And ever the shouts and screams of Christian and infidel cut strident across the thunder of the guns.

Then suddenly a white and blinding glare of lightning flamed in our eyes, and instant on its track came a terrific stunning crash that overpowered all other sounds, dwarfing them to nothingness, leaving us dazed. And with a swish and a roar came the rain, a very deluge, driving into our faces and blotting everything from our sight, and then continuous, without remission, the lightning blazed across the sky, the thunder crashed and rolled, shaking the very sea, blasting our ears to deafness.

For perhaps half an hour the storm endured, while still we fought hand to hand by the levin's glare, but presently the rain slackened and ceased, the lightning grew less frequent, passed into the distance, and the cloud-wrack parted, letting a silver moon shine through. I swam to the palisade, climbed up, and looked about, to see dozens of lifeless bodies floating on the water, the waves now beaten flat by the rain. But no living man could I spy, until at length one came swimming toward me. I gripped my knife in readiness, but as he drew near I saw that it was Xuereb; when we took the water, he told me afterward, he joined the party, unknown to me. An axe had got him on the shoulder, making a painful though not dangerous wound, and he swam with difficulty. I gave him a hand and lifted him to a pile, where he sat and panted, the blood running down his arm.

"Mother of God!" he gasped at length. "What a fight! What a fight! St. Elmo was child's-play to this! Are you hurt, Sir Richard?"

"By the mercy of God," I told him, "I have taken no wound."

"We are the last, it seems," he commented. "The others have died or betaken themselves ashore. Well, the commander should be the last to leave the field. But in this case you must grant me the honor, for I must rest a while."

"When you are fully rested we will go."

"Nay," he rejoined, "do you go now, Sir Richard.

212

It is not fitting that you should wait for a common soldier."

"Save your breath to swim with," I told him. "We go together."

"But—"

"It is an order."

And he was silent.

At length he spoke again.

"I can go now, Sir Richard."

"Very well." I stuck my knife upright in the pile, and slid into the water beside him. "Place your wounded arm on my shoulder and swim with the other," I told him.

He sucked in his breath sharply as the salt water took his wound anew.

"Sancta Maria, but that stings!" he exclaimed.

"Be comforted," I replied. "It will cleanse the the wound and cause it to heal by first intention."

"A blessing in disguise," he grumbled as we struck out for shore.

And so, side by side like brothers, we came to the rocks of la Sangle, where men with torches ranged up and down awaiting those who should return.

Don Antonio greeted me most effusively, as did all the garrison of St. Michael, our exploit seeming to them to border on those recounted in the books of romance. My first care was to parade my men, and the inspection showed that nine had been lost.

I do not know how much damage we did the Turks, but it was certainly far in excess of what we took, for I had seen in the moonlight more than forty bodies floating in the bay. Several of my men were wounded, but none grievously, and the washing in salt water proved most beneficial, for not a single wound festered; indeed, Messer Gaddi told me that it was the best possible treatment, seeing that the water was clean.

Don Antonio wrote to the Grand Master, vastly overpraising me and asking permission to keep me by him for a few days, a request which was readily granted. And with his reply la Vallette enclosed a personal letter of commendation which caused me to flush warmly with pleasure as I read it; beyond all question, our leader knew how to touch the hearts of his followers with generous and unstinted praise.

I remained for two days in St. Michael, for no reason I could discover beyond the fact that the commander enjoyed my company. I must admit, though, that it was no hardship to me, for Don Antonio de Zanoguerra was a most polished gentleman, who had traveled widely, knew many distinguished people, and could talk charmingly of what he had seen and done. Beyond this, he was an able and a gallant leader, and I was greatly flattered by the evident liking he had taken for me.

When the time came for me to leave, I crossed

the Bay of Galleys on a pontoon bridge that la Vallette had caused to be built—another proof of his
foresight, since ere many days this bridge was to be
the salvation of St. Michael. I reported to the
Grand Master, who welcomed me most heartily,
repeated his words of praise, and kissed me on both
cheeks.

"I did well by the Order," he said, "when I
snatched you from the grip of the Holy Office.
Would that all the Brethren had your cold daring
and your genius for leadership!"

"Nay," I deprecated, "it is but that opportunity
has come my way."

But la Vallette only smiled at this.

Sir Oliver Starkey, too, gave me warm greeting,
saying:

"I have stood sponsor for more than one Knight
of St. John, Sir Richard, but never one who has done
me more credit than yourself. It is a pleasure to
have you for my godson in St. John."

I could not help feeling that they overpraised me,
but my good Juan, who was present, later expressed
himself as disgusted with their remarks.

"The Grand Master did reasonably well by you,
I must admit—reasonably so. But Sir Oliver—!
One might think he was commending some school-
boy who had correctly translated 'Quo usque tan-
dem abutere, Catilina.' Praise, indeed!" he snorted.

"Nay," I expostulated, "that was high praise from him."

"If this be English praise, deliver me from English blame! But—" and he sighed "—I shall never understand you men of the north. I love you, though, Ricardo mio, even so."

"And I, you, my friend," I answered, gently, for in truth he was very dear to me.

"Of a certainty," he went on, "you are descended from some paladin of Charlemagne or Richard of the Lion-Heart. Never was such a man for thrusting himself into deadly peril and coming forth unscathed. Well, whither now?"

"I am on my way to pay a visit to our friends, the Lady Madeleine and the Countess Carmela. Do you accompany me?"

"Alas, I cannot; I must return to my post. Do you give them my compliments, and assure them that I am ever their most obedient servant." A mischievous smile played for a moment on his lips. "Would that I might be there to observe your meeting!"

"Why?"

"No matter." He waved his hand. "Forget not my message."

"I will deliver it," I promised, and with that we parted.

The Zerafa Palace lay not far from the walls of

St. Angelo, so had escaped destruction, and thither I turned my steps. After taking in my name, the countess' footman returned to assure me that the ladies would receive me anon, and I occupied myself with looking out the window until, hearing a step behind me, I swung about to face two fully armed cavaliers whom I did not recognize. I stared for a moment, trying to place them, then it dawned on me that these were the ladies I had come to see —they had exchanged their women's garments for men's clothing and armor. High boots, trunk hose, trunks, doublets, cuirasses, burgonets, and short mantles—from head to foot they were the complete cavalier, even to belted sword and dagger. Goggle-eyed, I stared in amazement, till at length the Lady Madeleine spoke.

"Do you not like us?" she asked, appealingly. "The Grand Master has given us permission to organize the women of Il Borgo for war, and that we might do it the more effectively, and have more freedom of limb, we have clothed ourselves thus. Some of the Knights were shocked, but the Grand Master and Brother William approved, commending our spirit and saying that true modesty is of the soul and has but little or naught to do with garb."

The countess laughed and wrinkled her nose.

"Don Diego was horrified beyond all measure,"

she said. "He gave us a sour look and a Spanish proverb:

" 'The wife who expects to have a good name
    Is always at home, as if she were lame.'
With that de la Mara spoke up. 'Nay,' quoth he, 'to describe these ladies one must use the second couplet of the quatrain:

   'The maid who is honest, her chiefest delight
    Is still to be doing, from morning till night.'
Thereupon the other Knights laughed at your friend Espinosa, and even the Grand Master vouchsafed Juan a smile."

But the Lady Madeleine was scanning my face anxiously for signs of disapproval.

"Richard," she said, timidly, and stepping close to me laid a hand like thistledown on my arm. "Richard . . . you do not think us . . . unmaidenly . . . you are not shocked . . . are you?"

Shocked! Never in all my life had I seen anything one-half so fascinating, so utterly adorable! A tress of her dark hair had escaped from under her burgonet and helped to frame the lovely oval face with its upturned eyes that sought my approval, its red lips that drooped in half dismay. Something stronger than myself surged up within me, and ere I knew what I was doing I had her in my arms and was kissing her soft, delectable mouth. Her arms went around my neck, her eyes closed, and she returned my kisses, so that my head swam and for a moment it seemed that Heaven itself lay open before me.

I was recalled to myself by the sight of Countess Carmela staring at me wide-eyed, spread fingers pressing over her open mouth. And with that I realized what I had done, and releasing the Lady Madeleine I stepped back a pace.

The countess recovered herself and giggled slightly.

"Oh, fie, Sir Richard!" she said, her voice trembling with mirth. "And you, who are betrothed in England! Have you a lady in Spain, as well? For I understand that you tarried there on your way to Malta. I have heard somewhat of David Evans' sweethearts—are all Englishmen like that?" And she giggled once more.

Her words fell on me like an icy douche—I was not formally betrothed in England, it is true, but my honor was engaged. For an instant the vision of the Lady Alice Chauntrey rose before me, then faded, and I knew the truth—I did not love her, and I did love Madeleine d'Armagnac. My feeling for Lady Alice, I now saw clearly, was but an infatuation born of her sprightly manner, her teasing ways; perchance but the fruit of propinquity; perchance the desire of every man for that which is held beyond his reach. But this was a far different matter; the Lady Madeleine's soul called to mine, her grave and loyal spirit matched my own, her sweetness, her sincerity—these were beyond and above all earthly desire; it was true heart calling to heart. And my honor was engaged in England!

Lady Madeleine knew what was passing in my mind; she read my face like an open page. Sudden tears overflowed her eyelids, and burying her face in her hands she fled from the room, while, aghast at what I had done, my head whirling, I stood and watched her go.

The Countess Carmela stepped near and took my hand with a gentle, reassuring pressure.

"My friend," she said, "I know what is in your thoughts, but do not blame yourself; the little blind archer is mighty, and will not be denied."

"I . . . I am dishonored," I muttered. "Unfaithful . . ."

"Pooh!" said she. "Sir Richard, I admire your sense of honor—but it can be overdone. Forgive me for teasing you; it was my thoughtless tongue that spoke, not my brain. I would not hurt you. As for the lady in England, surely she will release you when she knows—"

"But how can I tell her?" I almost wailed. "It cannot honorably be done! No, I must go away— never see the Lady Madeleine again—though I think it will kill me to do it," I added, dolefully.

The countess stamped her foot.

"Men are such fools!" she cried. "My husband was such another—oh, I loved him dearly, but he was forever prating of his honor! And in any case you cannot leave while the siege lasts." This much was true, certainly. "And in the meantime, we may think of some adjustment. Go now; I must go to Madeleine." And she fairly pushed me from the room.

I was glad of the countess' sympathy, but her talk of adjustment was vain; my honor was in pawn, and there was an end of the matter; the siege over, I must go back to England. The only hope lay in the chance that Don Diego might outshine me in distinction, but this, I knew, could not be. He had served honorably and well, it is true, but not outstandingly, whereas my exploits in the crypt of St. Lawrence, in St. Elmo, and at the palisade had brought me such renown that it was all but impossible for him to overcome so great an advantage.

I went to my quarters railing against the fates that had brought this wondrous prize to my hand, only to snatch it away ungrasped. For hours I tossed and turned on my bed, racking my brain to think of some solution. Lady Alice, I knew, would release me at once should I tell her the truth, but how could I bring myself to such a thing? I would be forever shamed, and must hide my dishonor in some deep forest of the Brazil or amid the snows of Muscovy, leaving behind me a name scorned by all true gentlemen. Madeleine, I knew, would share my exile, but could I ask her to? Never! I could not love a wife whom I did not respect, and though the philosophers all tell us that a woman's love is stronger than a man's, I could not ask her to help bear such a disgrace. Love is a marvelous thing, indeed, but life without honor is naught.

No, there was nothing for it but to return to a reluctant marriage and bear myself like a true gentleman, never permitting Lady Alice to suspect that she was not first in my heart. I groaned at the thought of the years that stretched before me, long years without the one woman of all the world, but there was naught else to be done; a gentleman may not cast off a maid who has promised him her hand.

True, I might seek admission to the Order as a Knight of Justice, taking the full vows, and thus be held excused from wedding the Lady Alice; nor could any reproach me, for earthly ties must ever yield to the service of Our Heavenly Father. And I believed that I would be accepted; my term and my labors at Malta might well be taken as compensating the period of probation. But this would bring me no nearer the Lady Madeleine, and though I should not be disgraced in thus evading a loveless marriage, yet I could not feel that I should be acting wholly as became a man of honor.

It was a hard problem, and offered but little prospect of enduring happiness. Undoubtedly there were many who espoused women for whom they had no love—being moved thereto by policy or money—but I could not feel myself at one with them; naught save honor could bring me to such an act. So I resolved that should I outlive the siege I would lay my doubts before my sponsors and the Grand Master, abiding by their decision. After all, I was not the first who must choose between love and duty, and it might be that God, in His kindness, would grant me some measure of comfort if I served him truly, even though it would not be such as I most desired. But almost I hoped that death would find me; the grave and the peace beyond would at least bring relief from this torture of soul.

The gray dawn was creeping in my window when at last I fell into a troubled sleep, to wake again to affairs which for a time drove all thought of love from my mind, replacing it with stern, immediate duties that brooked no divided allegiance.

CHAPTER IX

Of the Assault on St. Michael; and the Summons from Don Diego de Espinosa

SHORTLY before dawn of the fifteenth day of July, the bombardment ceased, and for an hour or more an unaccustomed silence reigned over the harbor and the siege works; our ammunition was running low, wherefore the Christian gunners also held their fire, that it might be employed against the attacking columns—also, that the guns might cool. Then, just as the sun pushed his rim above the water, a single cannon boomed from Mount Sceberras, another answered it from the landward side of St. Michael, and the Moslems launched a double attack on that fortress. The land assault was led by Hassem in person, and was repulsed after some hours of hard fighting, of which I saw little until the very end, the major part of my duty taking me elsewhere.

However, I had an excellent view of the battle of the Spur, and even came, before the day was over, to have some small share therein.

I was on the rampart of St. Angelo when the at-

tack by water got under way, and I have rarely if
ever seen a more beautiful sight. The early sun was
gilding in places the surface of the Grand Harbor,
which with its gently moving wavelets, stirred by
the morning breeze, seemed consciously to repeat
those famous words of Master Vergilius Maro:
"Splendet tremulo sub lumine pontus." * Though,
to be sure, the light here was from the sun, not the
moon. Athwart a portion of the harbor lay the
purple shadow of Mount Sceberras, and from its
base hundreds of small boats pushed out, their thousand oar-blades flashing, their gunwales low to the
water with the weight of fighting-men. The Moslems have no priests, such as we have, but there
are among them certain men whom they venerate as
holy, calling them mollahs, and in the leading boats
were a number of these, who seemed to be reading
aloud from some book—possibly the Koran, which
to these idolaters takes the place of our sacred Word
of God. There is no doubt that they were exhorting
the warriors, lashing them to the Satan-inspired
frenzy which they display in battle, but these mollahs did not join the attack; our guns had no more
than opened on the flotilla when the leading skiffs retired, and the fighting-men came on to the assault.

Some boats were sunk by our artillery and no few
of their occupants either slain outright or drowned,

* "The sea shines in splendor beneath the trembling light."

but the Moslems numbered such a horde that by
far the greater share pressed on through the storm
of missiles, endeavoring to force the palisade. This
proving too strong for them, they turned to the
Bastion of the Spur, whence our men poured a gall-
ing fire from cross-bow and from arquebus. From
the ramparts of St. Angelo all this could be clearly
seen, for the freshening breeze carried the smoke-
clouds down the harbor. A group of us gathered
about la Vallette and Sir Oliver, and from time
to time the famous optic glass was handed about,
that we might all have a close view of the desperate
fighting which went on. The land attack was somewhat hidden from us by the towering mass of St.
Michael, but so far as the Spur was concerned, we
were as favorably situated as the spectators of some
formal tournament.

When the Turks came to shoal water, they flung
themselves from their boats, wading ashore, then
rushed in countless swarms against the bastion,
shouting their war-cry of: "Allaho akbar!" Ladders were brought in great numbers, and an escalade
was tried, but the defenders, crowding the ramparts,
hurled down such quantities of stones, hand-bombs,
and fire-hoops that the ladders were broken and the
assailants driven back.

"For God and St. John!" rose the shout from
the bastion, and we of St. Angelo gave back a ring-

ing cheer. Somehow it pierced the roar of the guns, or so it seemed, for, looking through the optic glass, I saw the brave commander, Zanoguerra, turn and wave his sword to us. It may, however, have been no more than a coincidence, and we can never know.

Again the Moslems planted their ladders, again they swarmed to the attack, and now it seemed as though fate were against us, for the same thing happened as had occurred at St. Elmo—a spark found the magazine of ammunition. Our first notice of it was when a vast cloud of smoke rose from the bastion and mushroomed out above it, to be followed an instant later by the terrific roar of the explosion, while through the rolling, tumbling cloud we saw the hurtling bodies of men, their arms and legs asprawl, flung high into the air. Like a huge pall, the blinding smoke settled over the bastion, and when the breeze cleared it away a groan went up from us who watched; profiting by the screen of smoke, the momentary diversion, the invaders had planted their horse-tail banners thickly along the wall.

But Zanoguerra rallied his men and they fell on the Moslems with pike and sword and dagger, with battle-axe and mace. Long the fight went on, the Paynims striving to make good their footing on the rampart, the Knights to hurl them down, and we watched, tense and eager, as the battle swayed to and fro, and the din of shouts and cries and clash of metal was borne to us on the air. Higher and higher rose the sun, pouring down its tropic rays on the warriors, and the scirocco smote them with its fiery breath, straight from Afric's burning desert, but neither blasting heat nor wounds nor yet their own fatigue could halt the fighters; Christian and Moslem alike were fired by grim determination that took no count of pain or death. Once Sir Oliver, the optic glass at his eye, laughed aloud.

"I can see Brother Robert, the chaplain," he said. "He is rushing hither and yon, a crucifix in one hand, a sword in the other, the while he exhorts the Brethren and strikes down the infidel." Suddenly Sir Oliver's mirth gave way to an exclamation of horror and distress. "Zanoguerra is down!" he told us. "No, they raise him—he lies helpless in their arms—the Moslems rush to the spot—Just God, put forth Thy might; aid now Thy children in their hour of need!" And indeed we could see with the naked eye that the Moslem attack was growing fiercer, that the Christians were borne back, still fighting hard.

The Grand Master turned to me.

"Sir Richard," he said, "five companies are drawn up in the outer bailey, waiting to go as reinforcements. Place yourself at their head and lead them to succour our brethren. God be your sword and your defence! Go!"

It was no small honor to be chosen for so perilous a duty, and saluting, I departed at top speed. It was the work of a moment to call the men to attention, and we took our way at a brisk trot across the pontoon bridge that lay athwart the Bay of Galleys. As we went, I saw a Turkish reinforcement of ten great barges pushing across from the eastern slopes of Mount Sceberras toward the corner of the Spur nearest St. Angelo, and my heart sank, for they carried at least a thousand of the Yeni-Tscheri, and I knew that such a number of these troops must turn the scale; even the aid we were bringing would be overwhelmed. And I quickened my pace, to reach the endangered spot before this new swarm could master it.

But I had counted without de Guiral. There was a battery of sakers and culverins sunk almost level with the water, on the point beneath St. Angelo, and here that cool and gallant officer commanded. Seeing the Yeni-Tscheri set out, and seeing that their course would take them within range of his guns, he calmly waited until the boats, ignorant of his hidden battery, drew near, when he gave the word to fire. The first news I had of this was when an earth-shaking roar burst over the crackle of musketry and the din of shouts, and a great cloud of smoke bloomed out across the water, hiding the barges from our view. And when this cleared away I stood amazed at the frightful carnage, for one solitary boat was seen, pulling in mad haste for safety; the other nine were shattered and sinking, while far and wide the waters of the Grand Harbor were flecked with severed limbs, mutilated trunks, and bodies of the dead and dying. How in the name of Heaven could a single discharge of the guns spread such awful destruction? However, I had no time to ponder this, but must hurry to my task.

Reaching the bastion, I led my men directly into the fight, and shouting our war-cry of: "God and St. John!" we fell upon the Turks. The men of the Spur took heart when they saw our five hundred coming to their support, and though the infidels fought bravely they could not stand the shock of new troops striking in, and we drove them from the walls, hurling them in scores and hundreds to the rocks below. Some made their way to the shore, endeavoring to escape in the boats, but a sally from the bastion cut them off, and when they yielded and begged for mercy the Knights, having in mind the cruel slaughter of our brethren, gave them no quarter.

"Such mercy as you showed at St. Elmo!" cried our men, hewing the infidels down, and from this came into being the well-known phrase: "St. Elmo's pay."

Seeing the rampart thus cleared of their own, the Turkish guns across the water opened again on the Spur, and though they did in the main but little damage they brought about one sad loss. This was Don Frederick de Toledo, of whom I have already spoken. He and I, with von Helm, a Knight of the German langue, were speaking together on the wall, and had taken off our burgonets to wipe the sweat from our foreheads. Without warning, a six-pound shot struck Don Frederick full in the chest, throwing him some paces from us and killing him instantly. And a splinter from his cuirass pierced von Helm through the brain, so that he dropped and died without a sound. Thus in the moment of victory passed two good Knights; both excellent men, though von Helm was no such gallant and high-spirited gentleman as Don Frederick.

I had little time to mourn their loss, for a runner came from the landward side, asking aid.

"Hassem commands there," he said, "and is making head against us. Can you bring help, Sir Richard?" For with Don Antonio, Don Frederick, and von Helm all dead, I was now the ranking officer in St. Michael, or at least at the Spur.

I nodded, and bade my trumpeter blow the assembly, then when the men were gathered I told off a number to garrison the bastion in case of another attack, and led the rest up to the castle. Here,

flushed with fighting but not outwearied, we fell
like a tempest on Hassem. He found us no such
worn and spectral shapes as had defended St. Elmo!
No mountain torrent, fed by melting snows, ever
swept away sheep and cattle as we swept the base
infidels from the walls of our fortress. Down from
the rampart and down the slope we drove them,
slaying them in hundreds as they fled, and pursuing
them up to their very trenches—nay, had I not
sounded the recall, so hot were our men that they
would have followed the terrified Moslems right
into their own lines. But this I would not permit;
we were too few to plunge into any such maelstrom
as that would bring.

So we retired within the fortress, the men rejoicing in victory, while I acknowledged mingled
feelings; I was happy that we had beaten off the
attack, but my heart was heavy for Zanoguerra,
Don Frederick, and the other good men who had
perished. We had lost about two hundred altogether, including thirty Brethren, but against that
we might set, as nearly as I could judge, and including those slain by de Guiral's guns, between three
and four thousand of the Moslems. Should any
wonder at this great discrepancy in numbers, let
me say that there is a vast difference between attacking a walled castle and defending the same from
within the walls—especially when the assailants have

little knowledge of scientific warfare, but depend for success on sheer weight of men and guns.

That evening I sent the Grand Master a letter, telling the result of the battle and the present state of affairs, and shortly received from him an acknowledgment, in which he commended me highly and offered me the permanent command of St. Michael. Here was a compliment indeed, and my heart swelled as I read the words, but the matter demanded thought, and for an hour I shut myself up in the quarters of the late Don Antonio, while I debated whether to accept or not.

There was much to be said on both sides. For one thing, I doubted my fitness for such a post. I was unskilled in war, and the command of St. Michael called, it seemed to me, for a war-wise and crafty veteran. But on the other hand, la Vallette did nothing on impulse; his acts were invariably the result of cool and balanced judgment, and if he thought me fit for the place it must be that he could discern in me qualities which I could not perceive. Again, I was but an Associate of the Order, and there were on Malta many Knights of Justice, most of them older and more experienced than I was. Would not my appointment stir their jealousy? It seemed to me that it could not do otherwise. But here once more was a matter for la Vallette's decision; he knew the temper of the Knights far bet-

ter than I did, and if he deemed that I could hold
the post and not raise dissension in the Order it must
be so. But with it all, I could not convince myself
that he was right in selecting me. I had enjoyed
some success in a few enterprises, yes, but that was
by favor of God and by the help of good St. John.
Humility was enjoined on all the Knights—it
formed part of our vows—and what if pride and
arrogance in this new position should lose me the
favor of these Holy Ones? How great then would
be my fall! And even more, how great the disaster
to the Order!

In the end I wrote to the Grand Master, saying
that I doubted my worthiness of the post, and would
prefer to be with him in St. Angelo—nor was this
insincere, for there was none among us but de-
lighted to be in his company—but that if he commanded me to take charge at St. Michael I would
humbly and faithfully obey his orders. Back came
a letter:

"I commend your humility of spirit, my son, no
less than your high courage and your fidelity to
your vows. Be content; I would not force you to a
distasteful task unless impelled thereto by need.
Admiral de Monti will relieve you of the command,
when you may return to St. Angelo with all honor."

I have sometimes suspected that the Grand Master made this offer that he might determine whether

or not I would sin in arrogance, but in any case I am very sure that he would not have left St. Michael in danger.

On my way back to St. Angelo I met de Guiral, who clasped me to his bosom, saying:

"In very truth, Sir Richard, I love you like a brother! How you fell on the Paynim, beating them down as hail beats down the standing grain! It was a beautiful sight—beautiful! To my heart, comrade!"

And he hugged me again.

"Nay," I replied, "it was you who saved St. Michael. But for your guns, the Yeni-Tscheri had overpowered us; they are terrible fighters, those men —a pity they are not for the true faith instead of for Mahound."

"A pity, indeed. And the more since they are of Christian parents. Then you liked my gun-fire, eh?"

"Liked it! Never have I seen aught so joyous to my eyes, or so heart-lifting a spectacle, as when that smoke-cloud raised to show the broken barges, the scattered men."

De Guiral smiled gleefully.

"An excellent conceit, was it not, loading my guns with pieces of chain and fragments of metal?"

"Oh-ho! So that was it! I wondered at the destruction wrought by a single discharge."

"That was it," he answered. "Ma foi, round shot would never have done the work. I double-shotted the guns, then rammed down bags of chain and shards of broken metal. The infidels must have thought their patron saint the devil was loose among them!"

After some further conversation we parted, and I went on my way to St. Angelo, where I reported at once to la Vallette, who took me in his arms and solemnly kissed me on the forehead in public token of approval, while Knight after Knight drew near and clasped my hand, speaking generous words until I knew not which way to look, for very shame to be so over-praised. Even Don Diego came forward to congratulate me, though I could not feel his words ring true. Still, small wonder did they not, and I thought in my heart how ironic was our fate; he could not guess, nor might I honorably tell, how gladly I would resign to him the pretensions which had brought us both to Malta.

The ensuing day found both Turk and Christian laboring hard, the one to build up his attack, the other to strengthen his defences. Mustapha extended his line of entrenchments the full length of the promontory of St. Salvador, across the English Bay from the Bastion of Castile, thus completely surrounding both St. Angelo and St. Michael with trenches—on the landward side, that is—and since he already commanded the water, making it impossible for reinforcements to reach us. It seemed that his plan was to raze our walls by gun-fire, for he added sixteen huge cannon to the battery on St. Salvador, and these pounded night and day on the ramparts of St. Angelo and on the Bastion of Castile. Doubtless many will think that I exaggerate, but I tell the simple truth in saying that Messer Cassar's estimate was too small, for some of these basilicas were so enormous as to hurl stone bullets each weighing more than two full-grown men.

We were constantly at work rebuilding our ramparts where they were shattered by the Turkish guns, and the most perilous part of the labor was borne by Moslem slaves. This for two reasons. First, that the Christians might be removed from danger so far as possible, thus saving valuable lives for the defence; and second, in the hope that Mustapha might withhold his fire out of care for the lives of his brethren in Islam. This latter expectation proved vain, however, and it was only by free use of the lash, by cutting off their ears, and by more severe punishments, that we could drive the base creatures to their task. And more than five hundred of them perished from the artillery fire, thus proving la Vallette's wisdom in using them rather than Christians for this work.

The former inhabitants of Il Borgo, now many

of them refugees within the castle, and the soldiery as well, were constantly employed in breaking large masses of stone to a size convenient for dropping from the ramparts; in raveling large ropes and cables and filling bags therewith, for gabions; and in making hand-bombs and fire-hoops, especially the latter, they having more than once proved their worth. The artificers were busy making pikes, quarrels for cross-bows, and other weapons, and the women, organized by Lady Madeleine and the Countess de Zerafa, were as active and eager in the work as the men—why not, indeed? For the worst fate which could overtake us was death, whereas they, if captured, would end their lives in Turkish or Algerine harems, a fortune to which death were far preferable. It was a time vastly busier and more bustling than ever the days of peace, and with good reason, for the final grapple was not far off. Night and day, constant, unremitting, the roar of the guns was in our ears, the reek and stench of powder in our nostrils, while ever the sky glowed with that unearthly light, and the rock under our feet trembled with the concussion, and from time to time there sounded the rumble and crash of falling masonry. From the ramparts of the castle we could trace, far as the eye might reach, the enclosing lines of the trenches, stretching over hill and dale in a vast semicircle, with above them the leaping, spouting flare of the guns, so that by night we seemed wrapped in a great enclosure of lurid fire.

Throughout this perilous time, while both armies lay like couchant lions, making ready to spring at each other's throats, the Grand Master was everywhere about the works, going the rounds of the sentries by night, superintending our labors, advising, suggesting, encouraging the weary and the laggard, and heartening us all by his kindly smile, his serene, unflinching courage. He took no thought for his own safety, but exposed himself as freely as any common soldier, nor could we prevail on him to use due care.

"It is not for the commander to run such risks," we would say. "Will you not guard yourself for our sakes? What becomes of the body if the head is lost? Give your orders, and we will carry them out faithfully."

Then he would smile and shake his head, saying:

"How can I give orders if I have not seen with my own eyes what is needful? Nay, my children, fear not for me; I shall live as long as Our Heavenly Father requires my services. And when He no longer needs me, I am content to go."

Thereupon he would drive us, who lacked somewhat of his serene faith, to despair by walking out into that hail of stone and steel as calmly as though

239

it were but a summer rain, until for very shame none among us dared take cover from the storm.

During this period, la Vallette contrived to get word to the Viceroy of Sicily, begging yet again for aid, but still Don Garcia temporized, bidding us hold out another month, when he would bring sixteen thousand men to our relief. This well-nigh broke la Vallette's heart, for he saw that we could expect naught but false promises from that quarter. He wept when he read the letter, so that we who were present gathered close about him, reaffirming our loyalty and vowing to hold out while life remained within us.

"And," said de la Mara, "for my part, I ask naught better than to die for the white cross that floats above our ramparts. Soon or late, death comes to everyone, and happy is he who, dying, leaves behind him an honored name. Let there be no more talk of succour; if God requires our lives of us, I am happy to surrender mine into His gracious hands."

We all approved this speech, and la Vallette, wiping the tears from his eyes, vowed that no leader yet had ever known so gallant a body of followers as his own true Knights of St. John.

"I am an old man," he told us, "and the sands of my life run low. But I give thanks to Our Heavenly Father that He has permitted me to face my latter end in company of so goodly a band of worthy gentlemen. So be it; we will speak no more of succour; God and our swords shall be our aid."

And it seemed as though God chose this season to comfort us for the perfidy of Don Garcia, for the day following the receipt of the viceroy's letter we were called together in the chapel, when the Grand Master announced that a messenger had got through the lines bringing a letter from His Holiness of Rome.

"And," la Vallette told us, "His Holiness the Pope has decreed a plenary absolution for everyone, man, woman, or child, gentle or commoner, now engaged in this holy war against the infidel. Nor does this apply only to acts committed during the siege; whatever a man's past life has been, his sins are remitted, and he receives full pardon for all misdeeds."

Judge whether or not this heartened us! Nor was there any who did not strive with all his body and soul to merit this great reward.

The effect of the Turkish fire was now to be seen in more than one breach in our walls, so that we went in daily expectation of an assault. The Grand Master sent spies into the Turkish camp, some of them former Moslems who had accepted Christ, some of them our own men, but chief and most valuable was David Evans. This man had a genius for disguise, a perfect knowledge of Turkish customs and modes of thought, and, withal, a crafty brain. He was burned dark by many years of exposure to sun and wind, so had no need to dye his skin; as to hair and beard, many of the Yeni-Tscheri were even fairer than he was. And he wore his Turkish garments as though born to them, so what with all this, and his ability to ask questions without seeming to do so, he was able to bring us information of utmost value. At length, toward the end of July, he came back from an expedition with word that an assault was planned for the second of August, whereupon we made ready to give the storming columns a hot reception.

The attack came as predicted, Mustapha in person leading one assault against St. Michael, Pialé another against the Bastion of Castile. But so stoutly did de Monti and de la Mara defend their posts, and so savagely did the Christians fight, that for all their recurring charges the Moslems could not break through, and the westering sun saw them withdraw into their own lines, leaving the slopes and ditches thick-sown with trampled dead.

The following day, and each day thereafter, they came again to the assault, plainly intending to wear us down by repeated and persistent attacks, draining our strength away. On the sixth day they sprang a mine under the Bastion of Castile, destroying a large section of the rampart and pouring in vast numbers through the undefended breach. At the time, I was with the Grand Master and Sir Oliver on the wall, overlooking St. Michael, and the first news we had of the mine was when Brother William, chaplain of St. Angelo, came rushing to us, his eyes wide with terror, for he was inclined to be a timid man.

"The castle is taken!" he cried. "Take refuge in the inner citadel—it is the only hope! Flee, flee for your lives!"

"Life is a small thing," answered la Vallette, and not even stopping to don his burgonet he drew his sword and hastened to the scene.

There he found our men struggling furiously against the swarming hordes of Islam, while on the walls of the bastion there floated the great standard of the Crescent.

"To me, men!" shouted the Grand Master above the uproar of battle. "Now is the appointed time! Let us die together!"

Rallying to him, and with his flashing sword to lead us on, we smote the Turks so fiercely that we drove them back into the breach, clearing the bastion. But when we would have persuaded the Grand Master to retire into safety he sadly shook his head and pointed with his sword.

"Never!" he answered. "Not while that accursed

banner of Satan flaunts above our walls! That must come down, or Jehan Parisot de la Vallette will die in the ruin of his hopes."

Shamed, spurred on by his words, we charged again, with such fury that we drove the Moslems from the breach, tore down their banner, and rent it to a thousand shreds. Nor could the Turks be brought again to the assault despite the utmost efforts of their chieftains.

That night, however, ere we could rebuild our shattered walls, the infidels attacked once more, so that we fought in the weird illumination of the guns. But by the favor of God we beat them off, and in the morning la Vallette caused the Te Deum to be sung in the Church of St. Lawrence, and thanks to be offered at God's throne for our deliverance. This was to my mind the more heroic, since the Grand Master's beloved nephew, young la Vallette, had fallen in the struggle; as I had feared, his gilded armor made him a target for the infidel arquebusiers, and a bullet struck him down. Polastra, too, died in the bitter fight for the possession of la Vallette's body, and both were brought back to St. Angelo for honorable burial. But when we would have condoled with the Grand Master he shook his head, saying:

"All alike are dear to my heart; I mourn for Polastra and for the others who have fallen as I do for my own nephew. And after all, they have gone before us for but a little while."

I was not at the service of the Te Deum, being then occupied on an errand of mercy. About five in the morning, when we had driven the Turks from the Bastion of Castile, I felt a touch on the arm and turned to see Lady Madeleine at my side. I was shocked at her appearance, for she was covered with blood and dirt, and her face showed drawn and haggard, with dark circles under the eyes.

"Yes," she answered my look, "I have been in the fighting, and may claim to have done some service. My father taught me to use a sword, and I have not, I hope, disgraced his teaching."

"But you are wounded!" I cried, the very soul within me sick at the thought. "In God's name, let me take you to the chirurgeon. He should dress your hurts at once, that they may not fester—a green wound should ever be salved ere it grows cold. Oh, Madeleine, Madeleine!"

But she shook her head.

"Nay, Richard," she answered, smiling wanly, "this is Turkish, not Christian, blood. I am unhurt —but weary, so weary!

"However—" and she braced herself upright "—it is not to say this that I have been seeking you. Don Diego de Espinosa is sore wounded, and lies in the hospital crying aloud for you. He can scarce live till another sun, and begs most piteously that you will come to him. He claims to have done you a wrong, and despite his Holiness' indulgence he cannot pass without your forgiveness. And he fears that you will not come. But," she pleaded, "you will, n'est ce pas, Richard? You do not bear malice?"

I could not think what wrong Don Diego had done me; certainly our contest for Lady Alice's favor had been a fair one, and I ascribed his state of mind to the vain imaginings which so often beset a wounded man, or one near death. True, I did not like him, but this was no time for a Christian to let any mere personal dislike stand in the way of granting a dying man's last request, even though made in the delirium of fever.

So I assented, obtained leave from the Grand Master, and followed Lady Madeleine to the hospital.

CHAPTER X

Of My Wondrous Vision; of How Hamilcar Xuereb Lost His Leg; and the Letter from England

HAPPILY, no epidemic of disease had come to afflict us, and the only patients who were ill were some three or four sufferers from Malta fever, they having been in the hospital for months. But there were scores of wounded, both men and women, for the latter had borne their share in the fighting as nobly as their sons and husbands had done. So the hospital beds were full, and in the halls cots had been set up, between which we passed on our way to Don Diego.

"You will find him vastly weak," Lady Madeleine cautioned me. "And I beg that you will not tire him unduly. An arquebus ball has passed through his lung, and Messer Gaddi says that his end is nigh, but we would save him if it may in any way be done."

We found him at the far end of the building, in a special room set apart for the Knights, and the pillow on which he reclined was scarce whiter than his face, so much blood had he lost. He turned his dark eyes, deep-sunk in his head, on me as we entered, and a faint smile played on his lips.

"I take this kindly of you, Sir Richard," he said, feebly, and the faintness of his voice told me how weak he was. "I have done ill by you, and crave your forgiveness, that I may die in peace."

I took this for the hallucination of a wounded man, and replied:

"I am sure—" But he stopped me with a gesture of his fingers.

"Wait!" he said. "You do not know . . ." His glance appeared to be seeking something, and Lady Madeleine gave him to drink of some ruby liquid that stood on a nearby table. When he spoke again his voice was slightly stronger.

"You cold men of the north do not know what love is," he went on. "With us of the south it is a fiery, consuming passion that dwarfs all else. . . . From the first, I was determined that the Lady Alice should be mine; that by whatever means, I would clear you from my path. . . ." He paused for a moment, his face twisting in pain. "This is hard to say . . . nonetheless, it must be said . . . I it was who betrayed you to the Holy Office; I was the informer behind the celosia. That failed. . . . Then I bribed Calì to roll that rock on you in the first siege, but Xuereb saved you . . . Calì has since atoned his crime. . . ."

He was referring to an incident during the siege of St. Elmo, when a huge mass of masonry fell from the battlements, Xuereb barely pushing me out of the way in time. This was the first intimation I had received that the occurrence was aught but pure accident.

"But that—" I began, only to have him stop me again.

"Nay, there is yet more," he said. "I paid Casolani to put the poison into your food . . . but the dog saved you, and Casolani has atoned with his life. . . . I it was who instigated the raid through the catacombs, and contrived that Evans should hear of it; I knew he would take the word to you, and that you would volunteer. . . . I hoped that you might be slain . . . but your own foresight and hardihood protected you, and that also failed. . . . And it was my gun which found the magazine of St. Elmo . . . there, I think, it was God Himself Who cast the corner of His mantle over you. . . ."

I had listened with growing horror to this tale of treason, a horror which Lady Madeleine shared, for a glance showed her standing wide-eyed and white, her hands pressed to her bosom. But this last revelation was too much.

"God in Heaven!" I burst out. "You would have

destroyed the whole Order to free yourself of my rivalry?"

"Even so," he replied. "What was the Order to me, compared to the Lady Alice Chauntrey? . . . and I had my escape prepared. . . ."

"What else?" I demanded, harshly. "What other crimes lie on your soul?"

"That is all," said he. "And now that death is at hand, I fear to go unpardoned. Sir Richard, I cast myself at your feet, owning myself base and unknightly . . . and I most humbly beg your forgiveness. Can you grant it? . . . can you? I cry you mercy . . . my body is lost . . . I pray you, do not damn my soul!"

It was a piteous cry, but my ears were dulled by the swelling tide of rage that surged up within me, choking my speech. Of the noblest blood of Spain, how could he bring such disgrace on an honored house, than which none in all Christendom stood higher? And how dared such vile treachery, such treason in the dark, hope for pardon? And could I have overlooked the wrongs to me, what of the brave men who died at St. Elmo, blown to fragments in that terrible explosion?

I was frightened at the storm of anger which racked my bosom; it seemed as though I must fall on him and wring the life from him with my hands!

What agonizing death, what ages in Purgatory, what flames of Hell could pay for such foul deeds? False to his vows, forsworn, unknightly, an assassin—what torments could purge the sins from his black soul?

Shaken by my own violence, quivering from head to foot, I stumbled to the end of the room, where stood a crucifix, and there before the figure of our Savior I fell on my knees, praying for strength to master and control my rage.

As I knelt there a miracle was vouchsafed me, for slowly the wall dissolved in mist, then slowly the mist cleared away, and I saw before me a low hill, on its crest three stark crosses, each bearing a man, outlined against a dark and gloomy sky. I trembled with fear and awe, but slowly the figure on the central cross raised His head and looked at me, a smile of ineffable tenderness on His lips. He spoke, and low but distinct the words came to my ears:

"I forgave them that crucified Me."

Gradually the vision faded, and I saw again the tapestry on the wall, the stone crucifix on its pedestal. But for a moment I had knelt in the very Presence of Our Lord, and as the tears streamed down my cheeks I felt the anger leave my heart, driven out by a perfect calm and peace.

I got to my feet and returned to the bed, Don

Diego watching my approach with frightened eyes. I lifted his hand in mine and pressed it.

"You are freely and wholly forgiven," I said. "Go in peace, and may God forgive you even as I do."

The pain and terror were swept from his face, to be supplanted by a look of gratitude.

"This is most knightly of you," he whispered. "Most gracious . . . Sir Richard, I thank—" A cough cut short his words, a gush of blood burst from his mouth, and so his spirit passed.

I turned and went from the room, and Lady Madeleine would have accompanied me, but I shook my head. Vaguely I knew that men gave me greeting, but I paid them no heed, going straight to my quarters, where again I knelt, to give God thanks for His grace while yet that marvellous, that wondrous vision was fresh in my mind.

The ensuing days were bitter ones. Ringed about by savage foes, fighting by day and laboring on our defences by night, we got no rest save what we could snatch when exhaustion overcame us and we slept where we dropped. Night and day the guns roared, belching their shot and shell against the castle and the town, and dead and dying lay about the streets, while in our ears rang ever the groans and shrieks of wounded men and women. Again and again the hordes of Islam drove to the assault, but each time, fighting with the courage of despair, we beat them off, our women fighting bravely beside the men. Juan and I tried to persuade Countess Carmela and Lady Madeleine to content themselves with some less perilous task, but they only laughed at us.

"Are we not good swordsmen?" asked the countess, and I was fain to admit that they were, for what they lacked in strength they more than made up in agility and skill, so that more than one Turk came to his death on their rapier points.

"But no skill can turn an arquebus bullet," I reminded them, whereat Juan interposed.

"Let be, Ricardo mio," he said. "I withdraw my objections. Like the old woman with the pork, they have had a taste, and now their mouths water—for battle, not for bacon."

"A Roland for your Oliver, Juan," the countess chuckled, mischievously. "A proverb for your proverb. 'One cannot catch trout and keep his breeches dry.' And here—" she waved her hand toward the Turkish camp "—here are fat trout in plenty for the catching."

So we laughed with them, and gave over the attempt at persuasion.

Gradually our defences were crumbling under the bombardment, and it seemed merely a question of time when the Turks would sweep over Il Borgo and St. Michael as before they had swept over St. Elmo. Indeed, so perilous was our situation that the Council of Grand Crosses urged la Vallette to withdraw wholly within the citadel of St. Angelo, abandoning Il Borgo to its fate. But this the Grand Master flatly refused to do.

"Such a step would be ruin," he declared. "The cisterns of St. Angelo could never supply so great a multitude with water, and it is unthinkable that we should desert these brave men and women who have fought so stoutly for us, commoners though they are. No, my brethren, here we must make good our stand against the infidel, or here die for God and St. John."

Nor would he even consent to remove the sacred relics and the archives of the Order within the citadel, lest so doing cause the soldiers to lose heart.

David Evans continued his expeditions into the Turkish camp, and about the middle of August brought cheering news.

"A dysentery," he told us, "has broken out among the unbelievers, as was no more than to be expected, seeing that the foul beasts do not bury their dead, but let the rotting carcasses lie about in this gasping heat, to poison the air and the wells. It is carrying off hundreds each day, so that ere long Mustapha will have no army left. Well, God speed the day! Further, their provisions and ammunition are running low, the Sicilian galleys having cut off a number of ships which were bringing supplies. And several of their basilicas have been ruined by our gun-fire, and are useless."

"This last we knew," spoke up de Guiral. "We have missed their heavy shot for some days now."

Evans nodded, shifting his cud of the Indian weed to the other cheek.

"They are loading them on shipboard," he rejoined, "to send them back whence they came. Also, they are building movable towers, with intent to bring them near the walls and shoot down upon our ramparts. They—the towers—will contain falconets as well as arquebusiers. A brisk sally might dispose of them, I think, if made at night."

La Vallette nodded.

"It shall be cared for," he said. "Aught else?"

"They are mining in every direction under our defences," Evans went on. "God's truth, walking in Il Borgo is like treading on a honeycomb!"

"We have already started countermines," the Grand Master assured him. "Aught else?"

"Not at present," replied Evans. "More anon, if the luck holds."

The Grand Master rose from his chair and laid his hand on Evans' shoulder.

"You have done most excellently well, my son,"

he declared. "Should we come alive out of this peril, it shall not be forgotten."

A look of pleasure swept across the Englishman's face, and he knelt to kiss la Vallette's hand ere going back to his dangerous task. And dangerous it proved, indeed, for never since that day have I laid eyes on David Evans, nor has any word of him come to my ears. Whether some slip of the tongue betrayed him, whether he was recognized, or what befell him, I cannot say; only am I sure that here is another name to add to that long list of brave men who gave their lives for Christ and the true faith.

A sally disposed of the Moslem towers, and this attack I had the pleasure of leading; we had some brisk fighting, and set the torch to the great wooden structures. Also, there was some very hardy fighting in the bowels of the earth, when we broke into the Turkish mines, and here too, by the grace of God, we overcame the invaders, driving them back and breaking down their tunnels with well-placed charges of powder.

During one of these underground fights Xuereb was hurt, being caught under a fall of rock, and the following day he sent for me. I was at liberty, so went to him in the hospital, where I found him attended by Lady Madeleine, Countess Carmela, and Messer Gaddi, his wife being in tears outside the door; my good Xuereb was ever a favorite with both men and women.

"The chirurgeon tells me, Sir Richard," he explained, "that this left leg of mine is so crushed that it must come off above the knee. And I am told that the pain is so great in such cases that a man must be strapped to the table, and that the bystanders stop their ears against his cries. I would not prove a coward, and I bethought me that I might gain courage if you would stay by me and grip my hand. Would you consent to this?"

"Willingly," I answered, though in truth I liked the task but little; fighting is one thing, but to see pain inflicted in cold blood has ever sickened me.

"Nay," interposed Messer Gaddi, "I have here a device invented by the priests of ancient Egypt, to which I have given the name of 'anaisthesiant,' from certain Greek words meaning 'no pain.' I can assure you, friend Xuereb, that you will feel no pain whatever—from the operation, that is; honesty compels me to admit that there will be some in the healing, as from any such wound, but no more."

Xuereb looked doubtful, but Messer Gaddi called his assistants, who lifted the patient to a high table, then brought in a charcoal brazier in which were white-hot irons to cauterize the wound. Xuereb eyed this with obvious misgivings, and I saw him shudder. Also, the helpers brought in a great iron pot in which Messer Gaddi's knives and saws had been boiled, and taking the tools from this they spread them out on a clean sheet. Messer Gaddi answered my look of inquiry.

"A hobby of mine," he said. "I cannot tell why it is, but I have found empirically that there is less festering of a wound if I boil my tools. My professional brethren laugh me to scorn for it, but I stick by my guns. Now, good Xuereb, if you are ready."

Xuereb rolled a piteous eye on me, to which I replied with the most encouraging look I could command.

"Are you not going to strap me down?" he asked the chirurgeon, but Messer Gaddi smiled and shook his head.

"It is not needed," he answered. "Lift him up."

Xuereb was raised to a sitting position, and one of the assistants adjusted on his head a block of wood hollowed out to fit the skull. Stepping around behind the patient, Messer Gaddi took a heavy mallet and smote with calculated force on this block, and Xuereb slumped unconscious. Messer Gaddi and his helpers then flew at their task, working with incredible speed and deftness, and almost before I knew it the mangled limb was severed, the stump cauterized, and a flap of skin stitched over it, with bandages tied around. Xuereb was lifted back into bed, cold water was applied to his forehead and a drink of eau de vie poured down his throat. He drew a deep breath, blinked, then opened his eyes and looked around.

"Why am in bed?" he asked, dully. "Are you not going to take it off? And was it a shot that made the roof fall on me?"

Messer Gaddi laughed.

"It is all done, my good man," he replied. "We will get one of the artisans to make you a timber peg, and in a few weeks you will be stumping around once more."

"All done! But . . . but . . . I felt no pain! Beyond a slight headache, that is," he added, evidently astonished.

"I promised that you should not," smiled Messer Gaddi. "Say now, is not my anaisthesiant a success?"

"Sancta Maria, yes!" acknowledged Xuereb, scarce able even yet to credit the good fortune which had spared him the torture.

For myself, I was lost in admiration of the chirurgeon's skill, and told him as much. He received my words modestly.

"Each to his trade," he answered. "Yours is to harm; mine to heal."

"Sometimes," I resumed, thoughtfully, "I am inclined to think that yours is the nobler one."

He eyed me askance.

"Sometimes," he replied, dryly, "I am inclined to think that it is."

Xuereb was much depressed over having been ruined for his trade in the quarries, but I promised him that should we beat off the Turks I would see to it that he had a fishing-boat and nets, which he could readily use, wooden leg and all, and which would bring him in as good a living as the other. This comforted him, and he made an excellent recovery, displaying utmost gratitude to Messer Gaddi, and—with somewhat less reason—to myself.

It was evident to all that the heart was going out of the infidels, for their bombardment was slackening and their assaults were growing daily more and more feeble; it was with ever increasing difficulty that their officers could drive them to the attack. Even the Yeni-Tscheri manifested no great eagerness to come to grips with us, for which, remembering de Guiral's chain-loaded guns, I could scarce blame them.

"It has become a race to see which can endure the longer," said Juan to me, as we stood one day upon the ramparts. "We are like two weary dogs in one of your English dog-pits, each holding on in the hope that the other will give out first."

"If only the viceroy would bring aid!" I lamented, but Juan swore.

"Devil seize him!" he said. "We can do without him! Why should he come like the victor in a corrida de toros, to give the finishing stroke to a weary bull and claim the credit for victory? Ours is the heat and burden of the fight, ours be the glory."

Nevertheless, I was glad enough when, early in the morning of the seventh day of September, our hautboys rang out in a triumphant note, and hurrying to the ramparts we counted twenty-eight Christian galleys rounding the southern point of the island, and heard their guns boom thrice in salute. Eagerly we watched for them to attack the Turkish fleet, but they failed to do so, and our wondering hearts sank as they sailed away and were lost to view in the distance.

But we were not downcast long. Mustapha set to work forthwith, loading his guns and camp equipage and men on board his ships, and ere nones a runner came through the deserted trenches to tell us that the night before two hundred Knights of the Order and eleven thousand Spanish veterans had landed on the western shore of the island and were marching overland to our relief.

All that day and through the long night we watched the flickering torches, hearkened to the shouts and cries, while the Turks in mad haste loaded their galleys; and when morning dawned we saw them gathered in Marza Muscetto, ready for flight. Nor did ever music sound sweeter in human ears than when the deep-toned bells of St. Lawrence summoned us to Mass, to crowd the church and chant in unison with our gallant leader that glorious psalm of praise and thanksgiving, "Te Deum Laudamus—" "We praise Thee, oh God; we acknowledge Thee to be the Lord."

La Vallette, to be sure, deplored that the relieving force was not already at hand, that we might sally out, fall upon the infidels, and utterly destroy them. But for my part, I was content to do as Juan said—"make a bridge of silver for a fleeing foe." And it was with deep and sincere thankfulness— marred only by the thought of returning to England —that I joined with the others in the Te Deum.

One more slight skirmish took place, for Mustapha, conceiving that he had been too hasty in withdrawing, landed his troops to meet the relieving force. But the newcomers, under Don Ascanio de la Corña and the fiery Don Alvaro de Sandé (he who had commanded at the siege of Gelves) fell so savagely on the Turks that the infidels were driven into the sea and slaughtered there by hundreds.

Judge of the delight with which we greeted our comrades in the Order when they came riding into Il Borgo on the eighth of September, the day of the Nativity of the Most Holy Virgin! We ourselves were nigh mad with joy, but they were inexpressibly shocked at our appearance. And well they might be, for we showed haggard and worn, emaciated, filthy, scarred and wounded—some even pitiably maimed—and each and every one of us with armor stained and hacked and rusted. A sad contrast to their own spruce showing! For all that, though, we bore ourselves proudly, as well we might. Had we not, with nine thousand men, made good our home for four long months against fifty thousand of the very flower of the Ottoman Empire? Good cause we had for pride!

But all our hardships were forgotten as we clasped our comrades to our bosoms, then showed them over the fortifications, and to the accompaniment of their marveling exclamations told the story of that long and bitter siege. Briefly, we had lost some two thousand in all, including about two hundred Knights, and of the inhabitants of the island not less than seven thousand had been sacrificed by the brutal invaders. Our defences were in ruins, the towns of the island had been razed, and the crops destroyed. But against this we could set a fearful toll of Moslem lives, for more than thirty thousand infidels had left their bones forever on the island of St. John.

While I was chatting with a group from Aragon, a young English Knight came to me, saying:

"I seek Sir Richard Ayresford, and I am told that you are so named."

"In truth, I am he," I answered. "How may I serve you?"

He did not reply, but looked me over from head to foot.

"Well, sir?" I demanded, sharply, being touchy from the long strain.

"Your pardon," he apologized. "I meant no discourtesy, but I have heard somewhat of your exploits, and found myself overcome in the presence of so renowned a cavalier." This was handsome enough, and I relaxed. "I am charged with a letter for you," he went on, holding the missive out to me. "And likewise with one for Don Diego de Espinosa. Can you, of your courtesy, tell me where I may find him?"

"Don Diego is with God this month past," I replied, taking my letter and thanking the messenger. "Your pardon, gentlemen, while I glance over this?"

They readily excused me and withdrew a space, conversing among themselves, as I broke the seal.

"To the Rt. Worshipfulle Syr Richard Ayresford," ran the superscription, "Of the Most Noble Ordere of Kts. Hospitallers of Saint Johnne of Jerusalem, in the Isle of Malta, these by thee Hande of Syr Myles Talbote, Greentynge."

Within, I read:

"Dere Richard, itte grieveth Me sore thatte I shalle Grieve you, yet I doe truste thatte you shalle Pardone Mee, havying in Minde what goode Master Vergilius doth saye, namely, to wit, Varium et Mutabile Semper Foemina. To come atte the Truth, wythouten furthere Parleye, knowe thatt I am Wedde to Syr Jameys Fytzgeralde, whoe hath long Soughten my Hande in Maryage, I being most stronglye urged theretoe By My goode Father and bye my Ghostlie Adviser alsoe, whose Urgencie I mighte noe more wythstande. I praye thatt you will Pardone Mee, nor take thys toe gryvouslye toe Harte. I write lykewyse to Don Diego. Amm I forgiven? For indede Yoe are to mee more liken a Brothere, and I shalle ever cheryshe Yoe.

"Yrs,

"Alyse Fytzgeralde, Alyse Chauntrey thatte was. Given undere My Hande ande Sele, atte Fytzgeralde Halle, thys XVIII Daye of June, inne the yeare of Our Lorde MDLXV"

Three several times I read this letter, the first in stunned amaze, the second wondering, the third in sheer delight. For only with the last reading did it fully come to me what it meant, with all that it implied. Down from the ramparts and through the castle yard I strode, and straight to the palace of Carmela de Zerafa. Brushing aside the man who opened the door, I went to the drawing-room, where, as I expected, I found the Lady Madeleine d'Armagnac, with her friend the countess and Juan de la Mara. They were preparing to go out, but forgetting my manners, I gave them no greeting; merely thrust the letter into Madeleine's hand, saying:

"Read that!" Then I stood and waited while all three heads bent over the message.

Coming to the end, Madeleine let the parchment fall unheeded from her hand.

"Richard!" was all she said, and the next moment was in my arms, her arms about my neck, while in pure happiness she sobbed on my shoulder.

The countess plucked Juan by the sleeve.

"Come, my friend," she said. "I think we shall do well elsewhere."

But at the door Juan turned.

"Now may I sing the Nunc Dimittis?" he remarked. " 'Lord, now lettest Thou Thy servant depart in peace—' For at last I have seen Sir Richard Ayresford jarred from his habitual calm."

He waved his hand, and the door closed behind them, but opened at once, and Juan thrust his head in.

"I well-nigh forgot to tell you, Ricardo," he said, "that the Grand Master bids you wait on him this evening after vespers. He is minded to reward

" 'REWARD,' DID YOU SAY?" I ASKED.

you for your share in the siege, and to that end he
will himself stand your sponsor when you are received as a Knight of Justice, should you care to
take the vows."

I was staggered at this, for it was indeed a
mighty honor to have our adored leader, Jehan
Parisot de la Vallette, for a sponsor. And to have
him offer it himself—nay, it was all but unheard-of!
But was it an honor that I desired? In one way,
yes; but it would mean a vow of lifelong celibacy—
"to kiss no woman, not even a sister, and to hold no
child over the baptismal font. . . ."

I looked at Madeleine and smiled, and she smiled
back at me, a little tremulously.

" 'Reward,' did you say?" I asked.

Juan answered my smile rather than my words.

"I thought not," he laughed, and softly closed the
door.

AUTHOR'S NOTE

ONE of the most absorbing chapters in the world's history is that which deals with the prolonged struggle for supremacy between the Oriental and the Occidental civilizations.

The Oriental type of civilization is based on the individual as the unit of society, whereas the Occidental assumes the family as the unit. Though this may appear a very slight difference, it is not actually so, for it involves fundamental differences in mode of thought, social organization, religion, and general conduct of life. The Occidental type finds its highest religious development in Christianity, while Islam—more commonly called Mohammedanism—is the dominant religious expression of the Oriental type.

This struggle for supremacy antedates, in the beginning of its warlike form, any reliable historical records, and in this form extended to the battle of Lepanto, in 1571. One of its most interesting phases was the long-continued series of religious wars between Christendom and Islam, which ended with the Christian victory of Don John of Austria, and was marked by countless acts of outstanding bravery and self-sacrifice on both sides.

The siege of Malta, six years before Lepanto,

holds a deservedly high rank among the great sieges of the world, not only for the magnitude of the interests involved, but, more dramatically, for the steadfast courage displayed against tremendous odds, and for the many spectacular deeds of individual heroism which then took place.

In a historical novel, it is neither possible nor desirable to keep fact and fiction separate; if they are so separated, the story breaks down and loses its homogeneous character, the art of the writer being shown in a skilful blending of these two elements. In general, one may say that the main historical facts should be accurately related, but the personal adventures of the hero should be imaginary. To forestall possible requests for authorities, I would say that in the present story the accounts of the fight in the catacombs and the flight through them, though apparently historical, are fiction; the other main events can be found in various histories.

If I have failed to do full justice to this great siege, it is through no lack of appreciation or enthusiasm. But I do not feel that any words could do more than perhaps inspire the reader with my own admiration for the heroic devotion of the Knights of St. John, and especially their gallant leader. It is my sincere hope that I may at least have achieved that aim.

P. L. A.

East Orange, New Jersey

(1)